D0288478

FOREIGN BRIDES

Elena Lappin

FOREIGN BRIDES

PICADOR USA

FARRAR, STRAUS AND GIROUX
NEW YORK

FOREIGN BRIDES. Copyright © 1999 by Elena Lappin. All rights reserved. Printed in the United States of America. No part of this book may be used or reproduced in any manner what-soever without written permission except in the case of brief quotations embodied in critical articles or reviews. For information, address: Picador USA, 175 Fifth Avenue, New York, N.Y. 10010.

Picador ® is a U.S. registered trademark and is used by Farrar, Straus and Giroux under license from Pan Books Limited.

For information on Picador USA Reading Group Guides, as well as ordering, please contact the Trade Marketing department at St. Martin's Press.
Phone: 1-800-221-7945 extension 763
Fax: 212-677-7456
E-mail: trademarketing@stmartins.com

Library of Congress Cataloging-in-Publication Data

Lappin, Elana.
      Foreign brides / Elena Lappin.
         p.   cm.
      ISBN 0-312-26737-1
      1. Emigration and immigration—Fiction.   2. Married people—Fiction.   3. Immigrants—Fiction.   I. Title.
   PR6062.A67F67   1999
   823'.914—dc21   99-18684
                                                        CIP

First published in Great Britain by Picador

First published in the United States
by Farrar, Straus and Giroux

First Picador USA Edition: November 2000
10 9 8 7 6 5 4 3 2 1

FOR MY PARENTS

Contents

It was as if a curtain had fallen, hiding everything I had ever known. It was almost like
being born again.

Jean Rhys, *Voyage in the Dark*

FOREIGN BRIDES

Noa and Noah

Noa's decision to stop buying kosher meat, without letting her husband Noah know, was, on the face of it, a sudden impulse. One afternoon, on her way home from the park, she passed the butcher shop near her house, as she did almost every day. She had been thinking of the effort involved in making a special trip to her annoyingly talkative, nosy, and rude kosher butcher, the time it would take, the people she would have to 'bump into' while 'choosing' her usual cuts of lamb, chicken, and turkey (beef was no longer on the menu). The thought of it made her sick. Here, on the other hand, was a rosy-cheeked, cleanshaven JOE McELLIGOTT (as the red-and-white lettering above the shop's awning cheerfully announced) who displayed various pink sections of dead pigs in his window with such pride and delight that it almost made Noa's mouth water. So, she thought, what if I just went in there, pretending to be one of *them*, what if I just asked for a couple of broilers and some minced turkey – it looks the same, Noah will never know the difference. And if he doesn't know, he's not sinning. I am, but fuck that.

Not only did Noah not notice the difference – he was terribly pleased with that Friday-night meal. He actually loved the chicken, and asked Noa if she was finally using his mother's recipe. This was Noah's highest praise – he considered Noa's Israeli cooking unrefined. It used to upset her when he berated her culinary skills as if she were a kitchen apprentice trying to qualify for tenure as a wife. But now she thought, what can I expect from a debt collector?

When they first met, almost six years ago in Israel, Noah made Noa laugh by constantly referring to the similarity of their names. It didn't help that Noa pointed out the difference in the Hebrew spelling, and the fact that their names certainly didn't *sound* the same in Hebrew. His ended in a hard, guttural 'ch', which he liked to ignore; in his native north Londoner's English, 'Noah' dissolved in a nice soft vowel, and so did 'Noa', and therefore – he argued – they were meant for each other. It had been a funny joke until one night this red-haired British cousin of her best friend's stepsister took her to a decadent Tel Aviv disco, danced in a slightly drunken way, and then insisted on making love to her in his parents' empty summer penthouse.

Noa was intimidated by the chrome and glass everywhere. Her own parents' apartment in Ramat Gan contained mostly decrepit dark wood furniture, covered with dusty lace and musty-smelling polyester. Noah seemed sleek and intriguing to Noa. He talked incessantly in bed, which she found impressive; her Israeli boyfriends hardly ever uttered anything verbal except an occasional *ze tov?* She didn't understand half of what he was saying but it all sounded sweet, sexy, and somehow mysterious.

A few months later, she was starring in her own wedding video, though she didn't exactly remember signing the contract. His parents took over, there was a breeze of London in it all, her poor old Polish parents almost disappeared under the weight of so much chrome and glass and gold and diamonds. Finchley Gothic versus Ramat Gan Post-Holocaust Modern. Masses of dewy pale veiny legs on stiletto heels versus sun-devoured parched feet in sandals. Her friends didn't understand what she was up to, and neither did Noa – but it felt good. So she was giving up her life as she knew it, marrying a kippa-wearing accountant, moving to London. So what. She was twenty and he made her feel all grown up. And he sure didn't wear his kippa in bed.

The first two years were almost a success. Noa's English was so basic that she continued to be seduced by her image of Noah as a glamorous young businessman.

Their home in East Finchley, a family-owned property, seemed like a palace to Noa – though she felt uncomfortable with the decor, which was an almost exact replica of the Tel Aviv penthouse. To Noah's surprise, his brand-new wife was spending more time in the bathroom than in any other part of the house; for there, she could close her eyes in the blue-green bathwater and picture herself on the Tel Aviv beach. She felt like a trapped mermaid, escaping to her natural habitat.

Then one day she noticed that her English had improved so dramatically that she could enter into arguments with Gerda, her mother-in-law, and, although she didn't exactly win them, she didn't lose them either. Even better, Noa's ear suddenly started picking up occasional slip-ups in Noah's mother's accent; no matter how hard Gerda tried, her East End vowels kept showing in her unnaturally clipped speech, like the dark roots in her bleached hair. Noa, who had wanted with all her heart to feel close to her new family, was puzzled by so much unnecessary artifice, and now thought of her parents' home as refreshingly warm and unpretentious.

By the time she realized that Noah was actually employed in his father's business as a junior *debt collector*, and that his life's aspiration was to one day run the small Finchley office and become a *senior* debt collector, Noa was already pregnant with Noah's child. She had also by now finally deciphered and demystified her husband's sexy mumblings which invariably accompanied their love-making: the words Arsenal and Tottenham came up a lot, with very unsexy adjectives describing various players and plaintive remarks about their technique. When she had first grasped this incredible fact, Noa simply asked Noah why he had to think and talk about football during sex. He had answered, without the slightest hint of embarrass-ment, that he thought about football *all* the time, and saying his thoughts out loud during sex helped him slow down. Noa was so flabbergasted she forgot to ask which team he supported – though she had a strong feeling it was Tottenham.

And what did Noa think about in bed? Initially, close to nothing. She tried to slowly get to know Noah, whose way of life she had accepted so blindly, without worrying about the fact that he was a total stranger to her. So she did what she had done from the day they met: watched him, watched his every movement, listened to his every word. As long as Noah remained an enigma, he was worth every boring minute of her boring life with him. He was safe. But the minute she cracked his code, he was finished and didn't even know it.

'Noah,' she said one evening after putting their son to

bed. They were lounging around in front of the TV, without really watching anything. 'What does a debt collector actually do?'

Her husband of five years looked up from the sports page of the evening paper and stared at Noa. She repeated the question. 'We . . . we make people pay their debts,' he said slowly and gave her a hard look she knew well. It meant: shut up and leave me alone. Not this time; Noa was on a roll. 'But how? Are you some kind of police or something?'

Noah sighed. 'Course not. We just write letters and tell people what will happen if they don't pay up.' He was dying to go back to his paper. Noa's inquisitive mood was beginning to annoy him. And she was exposing her ignorance about things everyone knew and no one questioned. Thank God his parents weren't there to hear.

'So what are you?' Noa's next question startled him. 'Some kind of mafia?'

Noah's eyes narrowed just a bit before he said, his voice louder than usual: 'No, we're not. Of course we're not. But we *are* licensed to send in the bailiffs and initiate court orders if the client doesn't cooperate.'

Noah knew how to keep cool, very cool. Even under a lot of stress. He knew how to sound menacing and detached at the same time. Maybe it went with that strange job of his. But Noa smelt defeat in the air, and it wasn't hers. 'So, Noah,' she persisted, emphasizing the 'ch' sound which she knew he hated, 'I still don't see it. How do you get people to pay their debts? And why do you do it? Are you evil or something? I think you are. You and your father. But you're worse.'

Noah searched his wife's face for a trace of a smile. Anything to indicate that she was joking. Whenever Noa said something weird, which happened quite often, he made excuses for her on account of her underdeveloped Israeli idea of humour. Like her cooking, Noa's sense of what constituted an acceptable remark was frequently on the clumsy side. Noah was tired. He hated his job. He hated the life he had forced himself to lead. He was beginning to hate his gorgeous, awkward, crazy wife.

'If you are trying to be funny, give it up. You have nothing to say, as usual. And you can't hurt me. I'm going to sleep.'

Noa was a good aim. She had been a first-rate shot in the army. The remote control she threw hit Noah between the shoulder-blades. He turned around, raving mad. The Armenian candlestick hit him in the balls. He doubled over, gasping for air and cursing. 'You bitch. You fuckin' bitch. Go to hell.'

Noa slid off the couch and reached for Noah's red

mane, gingerly. He tried to bite her arm, but she gave him her mouth instead. For the first time ever Noah forgot his football mantra.

Later, while he slept, Noa went into the bathroom to cry. But I *did* mean it, she thought. I meant everything I said, and I meant to hurt him. I need him to go back to being the stranger I fucked. But with me in control this time. You owe me, my little debt collector, she whispered almost tenderly, climbing back into bed. It's pay-up time.

After that night, their daily routine returned to normal, seemingly unchanged. Noah's life continued to revolve around his father's office, football, and dutiful socializing with his parents on weekends and holidays. Sometimes he craved Noa's body, though not her thoughts. Noa couldn't care less. She had a plan. Dressing their son mostly in red and white (Arsenal colours) was only a small part of it.

It began with that visit to Joe McElligott's butcher shop and her first purchase of *treyf* chicken. She had intended to be in and out of the shop as quickly as possible, to avoid being seen by a friend or acquaintance of Noah's family. But she was delayed by two things that caught her eye, almost simultaneously: Joe McElligott's attractively bulging biceps under his white, slightly blood-stained T-shirt, and the sign on the cash register saying WE DELIVER. He smiled at her and said something flattering about her lovely French accent. She smiled back without correcting him and made a mental note of the price list on the wall. She would save a lot of money by sticking to *treyf*. 'Yes, ma'am, I do the deliveries myself these days. No charge. Call us any time.' His plump cheeks reminded her of her son's smooth round *tusik* . . . She took the business card he offered her and nodded. Joe McWhatever, she thought, pushing the stroller outside, guess what. This French customer wants your meat.

The phone rang as soon as she unlocked the door. 'Noale,' her mother said softly, as if she were in the same room. 'I don't know what to do. Your father . . .' 'What??! What happened to him?' Noa screamed. Does the punishment system work *this* fast?! She hadn't done anything so far except *think* about it! 'Nothing, nothing happened to *him*. It's what happened to *me*. He has another woman, that's what.' Noa was numb. This didn't make sense. Her parents were in their late sixties, and everything about them was as predictable as the pattern on her net curtains. They were both survivors, from the same small Polish town. They've known each other since they were almost children. Now they were old, wrinkled, their health was precarious. Their lives had been unspeakably hard, and their worn-out bodies showed it. They couldn't possibly feel desire for other people and *their* bodies!

'I don't know what to do, Noale. You know the beach we drive to every day?' Noa's parents belonged to the daily contingent of determined old men and women who exercised on the Tel Aviv beach early each morning. She had watched them sometimes. Their leathery skin shook in tiny ripples as they marched in and out of the cold waves and performed old-fashioned callisthenics on the sand. 'The Russian woman we befriended? The one that had those bruises from her husband. The shikse! I invited her to my own home and gave her my old dishes and a kitchen table! My own dishes! Call me back, we can't afford this.' Noa called back and listened to her mother weep, long distance. First quietly, like a little girl who lost a precious toy, then louder and louder until her wail sounded like an ear-piercing siren, or a mother mourning the loss of her child. 'Do you need me there? Do you want to come here?' Noa asked, gently. 'I don't know yet. I have to think. Kiss the baby from me. Call me next week.' She's *not* falling apart, Noa thought, amazed. She wants him back!

For some reason, she decided not to tell Noah. She could just hear his feeble jokes about her father the geriatric philanderer. As she unwrapped the pale, moist chicken, spreading its juicy thighs, a horrible image of her father humping a fleshy, hairy Russian lady flashed through her mind. She could only picture his penis as a kind of insemination syringe, not an instrument of pleasure. Come to think of it, she couldn't picture it at all. She rubbed a thick layer of spices and sauces into the skin of the cold chicken, to hide its true identity, and shoved it in the oven. Don't let me down, she said to the dead bird. Act kosher.

Noah's parents dropped in the next day on their way home from shul. Gerda was stunned by her son's praise of Noa's chicken, and insisted on tasting the leftovers. Noa was a bit worried but did not resist. Gerda tasted, swallowed, approved. With a slight tinge of envy, she asked her uncouth daughter-in-law for the recipe. Go to Joe McElligott's in the High Street, Noa felt like saying. He'll inspire you.

After that, it was a cinch. She would call Joe with her order, and he would deliver. At first, only once a week. 'Thank you.' 'You're welcome, ma'am. What a cute baby.' He was a bit of a chef, and they started talking recipes. She discovered that Noah loved the food she prepared according to Joe's suggestions. There was the semblance of peace in their home. They were a happy dysfunctional family. Just like everybody else they knew.

Joe's biceps continued to intrigue her. Sometimes she watched him, unseen, through the shop window, chopping and slicing masses of bloody animal corpses, his muscular right arm a vigorous extension of his powerful body. At home, when she dug with her hands into the raw meat she had bought from him, she felt a wave of lust for her new butcher. One day she lingered a little longer than usual in the window, until he looked up and saw her. Their eyes interlocked for a brief moment, unsmiling. Two hours later, he brought her order, four days too soon. She dumped the meat on the kitchen floor and took him straight to her bedroom. Afterwards, Joe tried to thank her in basic French. Noa giggled and told him the truth.

Joe sat up in her and Noah's bed, which seemed to have shrunk in size. 'Ah. So *that's* why you never buy my pork. I've been wondering.' He gave Noa a great recipe for roast turkey and promised to bring an Arsenal hat for Noa's little boy. Next time.

Noah loved the turkey and failed to detect another man's scent in his bed. He did, however, object to the hat when it appeared on his son's head. 'Noa, Noa. Don't you know *we* support Spurs? Get rid of that thing.' But the baby screamed when he made an attempt to grab the hat, and so it stayed, to be followed by a little Arsenal T-shirt and jacket. Joe was a fan.

Noa loved what happened almost every time Joe came to her door. It never lasted long – it couldn't – but it was perfect. They were lying to the world, but not to each other. They were strangers on the outside, but not in her bed. The polar opposite of the life she led with Noah. She even loved Joe's work; she called him her butcher from heaven.

She had been expecting her mother's call, but not this: her mother wanted to come to London and stay with Noa until her husband came to his senses. How long? A week, a month, a year – as long as it takes. 'I'll show him, Noale. He can have her but he can't have me as well. I want to live too. Like you. Kiss the baby from me. See you Friday. Can't wait.'

Gerda's call a few minutes later gave her a chill. 'Noa, have you switched butchers? Mr Meyerson has been asking for you. He says he hasn't seen you in ages! *Where* do you get your meat these days? Not Shmulik's, I hope? He's a real *ganef*. You should have asked me first!'

Noa lied, with great skill. No, Gerda. Not Shmulik's. And changed the subject, no less skilfully, to her mother's visit. 'This Friday. Well . . . it's my father. He's been cheating on her. Can you believe it?'

Gerda could hardly conceal the excitement in her voice. *This* was juicy. Didn't think the old Weinstock had it in him. She offered solicitous advice and said she'd come and stay with the baby while Noa went to Heathrow to pick up her mother. Noa thanked her and accepted.

And so it happened that Joe knocked on Noa's door,

his usual meat delivery in hand (with a few pork chops thrown in this time to introduce his favourite customer to a new delicacy), and found himself face to face with Gerda. She gave him a stern look and asked who he was. 'McElligott the butcher, ma'am,' said Joe, a bit taken aback but still smiling – and why not? As far as he knew, their affair was a sweet secret, and Noa had told him nothing about her subversive anti-kosher activity. He left the parcel with Gerda and went, a little surprised at Noa's absence, but not too worried.

Gerda carried the meat into the kitchen, moving very very slowly, like a stunned animal. Had she heard right? *McSomething?* A *goyish* butcher? This could not be. She unwrapped the package and let out a primal scream. It had to be a mistake. But Noa's name and address was on the invoice she found attached inside. This Israeli par-venue was feeding her son *treyf!!* She had always known there was something strange about her. And that father of hers! And her poor boy! Suddenly, Gerda remembered the delicious taste of Noa's chicken. She shuddered. She wanted to scream again, and call Noah, but instead she cried and cried, until she fell asleep, exhausted, on the living-room couch.

On the way home from the airport, Noa listened to her mother's stories about 'that man' and 'that woman'. But he's still my father, she thought, how do I tell her that? And it seems I have more in common with him than I ever knew. Suddenly she saw her father's gentle face, remembered his shy smile and his kind eyes, his slow, awkward gestures when he tried to hug her. So what if his still barely erect body had a life of its own. Everything was so goddam complicated . . . 'Oh, I love this English rain, Noale. I'll stay a while. Let them bake in the heat.'

When they arrived, Noah was already there, summoned by his mother. Gerda, without acknowledging Noa's mother's presence, grabbed Noa by the sleeve and pulled her into the kitchen. 'This!' she hissed, pointing at the meat with a mixture of moral outrage and physical nausea, 'this you've been feeding us! Who are you, the devil?'

Noa was expecting some kind of explosion someday, but not so soon. Not today, not like this. Gerda wasn't supposed to have the upper hand. She looked around the living-room. Noah's face was white, even more than usual. He was speechless. Noa's mother was confused. She didn't understand what this was about, but she did register Gerda's rudeness and barely contained violence. And the defiant look on her daughter's face.

Observing what was about to become a scene of carnage, Noa regained her courage just as quickly as she had lost it. Strengthened by months of cheerful lovemaking with Joe, she suddenly felt like facing the enemy instead of wallowing in hidden pain. She would leave the collecting of debts to these pitiful characters, she decided, with their ugly penthouses and their phoney accents.

'I've been meaning to tell you,' she said without a trace of hysteria, looking straight at Noah, 'I'm not staying. Not if it means living like this. Like your parents. You're an *efes* . . . And . . . your team is crap.'

Gerda jumped up and offered to throw away the meat, but her son stopped her and asked both mothers to take a walk. When they were alone, Noah collapsed on the sofa and burst out laughing: 'Noa. Come here. You idiot. I never eat kosher away from home. I really don't give a shit. I do these things for *their* sake, but I don't give a shit. Didn't you know? Really and truly. You can buy any meat you want as far as I'm concerned. What's for dinner?' He reached for her, but there was a knock at the door. Joe had come back, hoping to find Noa alone this time. Instead, she was with her pale-looking, panting husband. Noa made a step towards Joe, but her son preceded her. He ran to him, waving his little arms and shouting 'Ah-senal! Ah-senal!'

Some debts are not worth collecting, thought Noah, noticing the wistful look Joe gave his wife. 'Wait!' he said quietly as Joe turned to leave. He disappeared into the kitchen and quickly returned with the meat parcel. 'Please take this back. My wife and I are becoming vegetarians. As of tonight.'

'And I'm cooking,' he added when they were alone again. 'Do you feel like pasta?'

Noa nodded. She wasn't sure who had won this one, and she didn't care. It was over, and it felt good. She decided to buy little Gili a Tottenham hat.

Black Train

There is no easy way to say this: if my mother hadn't shat herself that New Year's Eve, in a state of sullen drunkenness and in full view of a large melancholy party marking the end of 1968, we would never have left Prague. While so many of my friends' families were packing up and leaving, or, more often, leaving without a great deal of conspicuous packing, my parents refused to budge, Russians or no Russians. Until that festive night, when the unbearable embarrassment of suddenly finding herself sitting in a small brown puddle of her own making forced my mother, with my father and myself in tow, to leave Prague on the first train to Vienna the next day, never to return. Our half-hearted pleas that 'she fell asleep and it wasn't her fault' made no difference: losing control over her own body was, in her eyes, the worst weakness of all. No one would ever forget what she had done; she *had* to emigrate.

She had a point, as Dr Poussard would say. My mother

was a great actress, much loved and respected. Having started out, in her teens, as the equivalent of a radiant Hollywood ingénue in bleak socialist realist films about badly dressed people in dusky fields, shadowy factories and cruel maternity wards, she gradually matured into major roles on the stage and in the nascent new wave of Czech cinema. I was proud of her. She didn't leave much space for my father and me, but we didn't mind. Not really.

My parents discovered each other, unromantically, on the set of one of those early drab films; my very young mother was trying to outshine the rest of the cast which included my father as a patriotic poet and swarthy coal-miner. The funny thing was that my father had, in fact, been both before he took up acting. And his hair was, in those days, literally coal black – as was mine until about ten years ago. After he married my mother he continued to play small but solid film parts, but, technically speaking, his main role in life was to act as a barrier between her high-strung excitability and my slow-motion responses to all that over-stimulation. He was like a sensitive thermo-stat, installed to regulate the temperature of our tiny but intense family. No wonder he broke down so soon after we left our home. This is Dr Poussard's insight, not mine. Although I did help him by remembering that my father cried a lot on that train to Vienna, and when he stopped he wrote a very long poem, beginning with the words 'We might as well be dead'.

The poem is called *Černý vlak* (*Black Train*), and I encouraged him to publish it in a Czech exile magazine in Toronto. And I'm glad I did, because it made him sort of famous, for a while, among the Czech Canadian expatriates. He survived only two of our Ottawa winters, but because of *Black Train*, his final sadness was sweet, not bitter. Now that's *my* insight, not Dr Poussard's.

I was almost fifteen when we left Prague. Intellectually pretty precocious, but physically . . . Suffice it to say that I was still waiting for my breasts to grow. Unlike my best friend Olina, who had the works by the time she was fourteen, including several cheerful attempts to lose her virginity. Olina lived one floor below us, in a huge apartment with her parents, two grandmothers and hardly any furniture. She was an only child, like me, but unlike me, she grew up in a safe cocoon of even tempers and quiet apathy. Also unlike me, she modelled herself on my mother's wild ambition and sometimes regal, sometimes brittle manner, whereas I secretly longed for Olina's sturdy, gentle mother, with her firm hugs that always smelled of sugary Christmas cookies. As it happened, Olina stayed in Prague and became a film star. Her parents quietly moved all our antique furniture and paintings into their apartment after we left. They sent us most of our books and photo albums but my parents never forgave them for inheriting the intimate contents of our Prague home. Still, Olina and I stayed in touch, even though I never had much to report as I disappeared deeper and deeper into American suburbia.

The party had been at our apartment. Most of the guests were actors, writers, singers, artists, film directors. My mother's crowd. Olina was there too, because her parents were always invited to our parties, ever since we were babies. Not because they were great friends – they weren't – but because my parents liked the idea of being good neighbours. Olina's parents never had parties.

Dr Poussard often stresses the fact that it was Olina who first noticed the smell, and informed her parents that my mother was asleep in a pool of liquid shit. Olina's voice had a lovely, resonant ring to it. Still does.

But it wasn't the sound of Olina's voice that woke my mother, it was the sudden silence in the crowded room that grew and spread like a drop of ink on tissue paper. When she realized her situation, she sort of died. Not outwardly – her manner was as grand as ever, and she even had a convincing go at amusing self-mockery. But when we left, she took that silence with her to Vienna and later to Canada, propped it up like an invisible wall and never again looked beyond it.

Our emigration was a comparatively smooth, if improvised, affair. I don't remember how or why we ended up in dreary, frozen, freezing small-town Ottawa, but it was a fitting punishment for two people – my parents – who didn't want to be reminded of the life they left behind. Yes, it was a suicide of sorts, and I don't need Dr Poussard to tell me that.

After a lifetime of what I would, even now, describe as supreme material and even spiritual comfort, we were suddenly poor, in every sense. We knew that as time went by, our native language would ossify, and our painstakingly acquired English would always feel like snow falling on ice-cold skin.

My father's depression set in as soon as we boarded that train to Vienna, but didn't really begin to show until we were settled in Ottawa. Our first home there, on the tenth floor of a tall red-brick building, was a small apartment with a picturesque view of the Rideau Canal. We liked that fresh, misleading impression of a white idyllic town, with smiling, red-faced people mindlessly skating up and down the canal. We liked the cosy warmth *inside* every covered space. But within a year, we realized that we'd ended up in a place which was not a fun foreign playground. It was a real country we were supposed to call home, and couldn't.

While other Czech exiles we knew were swiftly moving into this or that niche of Canadian life, my father sat at home writing long poems. When the words stopped coming, he would weep, his face buried in a large Czech thesaurus.

Needless to say, my mother never acted again. She got a job teaching Czech to Canadian diplomats; every year, there would be a few who needed tutoring in preparation for their posting to Prague. My mother turned out to be a gifted teacher, very much in demand. Her part-time salary was our only income. I didn't mind, because all I did for the first two or three years of my new life was watch sitcoms, in the safety of our self-imposed hibernation.

And that, I think, is pretty much all I should have to explain about who I am. The rest is insignificant and ordinary. Even Dr Poussard would agree. All émigrés have the same basic story to tell: there is that small death when they leave their home country, there is that short-lived euphoria when it looks like they've been blessed with a chance to rewrite their script in a free society, and then comes the life-long sadness once they realize that they have made an irreversible choice to cut themselves off from their roots. They can appear successful and lead exciting lives – but they will always feel like second-class citizens, wherever they are. And that huge void inside will never, ever be filled.

So that's what happened to me. When I was left alone

with my mother, I was finally forced to crawl out of my shelter and face the world. Luckily, I had turned into a pretty attractive young woman by the time I was ready to *be* a woman, and if you didn't know my history you could mistake me for a happy-go-lucky Canadian girl. I didn't do anything unusual at all: studied English Lit at Ottawa University, travelled all over Europe and the States, and didn't really know what to do with myself after that. When I met Jimmy D'Angelo from Valhalla, New York, I wanted to have a home with him.

Jimmy was the most stunning-looking young man I had come across in real life. He could have taken Hollywood by storm, but he chose to be a plumber in his father's business. I loved him because he never worried about my past. Couldn't read my father's dark poetry. Didn't see my mother as a tragic *grande dame* of Czech film and theatre, but as a lovable if slightly difficult ageing lady with annoying demands and a funny accent. Not too different from his own mother and grandmother (both called Lucia).

I also loved him because his ancestors were rugged stonemasons from Tuscany who had come to build the Valhalla dam, and now his entire clan lived near us in Westchester or in Brooklyn. I had an instant large extended family, and with my dark hair I looked like one of them. Even my name now sounded almost

Italian — Anna D'Angelo. Much better than Anna Kotrlík.

Jimmy was earning vast amounts of money. His name seemed to be at the top of every Westchester housewife's list of plumbers to call at the slightest excuse. His card, I was sure, was embossed with their mental image of my divine-looking husband crouching under sinks and toilets, extracting unspeakably intimate *things* from the invisible insides of their houses. Or was that my image of him? Jimmy was, as Dr Poussard once put it, a natural man. This was his way of saying that I had married a primitive hunk, a man with whom I could not possibly have anything in common. He couldn't imagine us having a proper conversation.

He was wrong. I loved talking to Jimmy; he was like a warm bath. And that was exactly what I needed — someone who didn't *need* to know everything about me, only the easy stuff. Plus, he was the only person I ever told about my mother's dark secret. In fact, I think I told him on our first date. His solemn dark face quickly dissolved into a soft, understanding smile, and I knew he would never say a word about it. I also felt, instantly, that my father would have loved this guy.

Jimmy had a little dark secret, too. He was trying to write a story, just one, from the time he was sixteen years old. He had once had an English teacher, Mr Weiss, who had encouraged him to write and to go to college, but Jimmy didn't, and this story was his way of proving to himself that he could have, if he had really wanted to. He never got past the first two paragraphs, and when he showed them to me, I was really impressed:

I had so many sisters that there were days when the house positively reeked of menstrual blood. Though I never actually *saw* their blood, I had a permanent picture of it as a vile, thick, muddy liquid, not red but black. Occasionally, I had dreams of wading through swamps of it, slowly, with difficulty, until I would lift my feet into the air and just fly above it, like a big clumsy bird.

I felt sorry for my sisters. Often, several of them would lie curled up in various parts of the house, craving relief from what seemed like very painful stomach cramps. I imagined the interiors of their bodies, the hidden caves and crevices and mysterious mechanisms of un-fertilized eggs seeking an exit, causing all that haemorrhaging. And while my sisters suffered their monthly pains, I walked among them like a young male god, free and unhampered by any unpleasant reminder of my sex.

According to Dr Poussard, Jimmy was simply writing the equivalent of a journal. Well, Dr Poussard's opinion doesn't count when it comes to literature. I happen to know that Jimmy had an ambitious plan for that story: his narrator was a deaf and dumb serial rapist. It was based on a school friend of his, a boy called Tony Galante, who was serving a life sentence for gruesome rapes he committed on the Metro North train line, usually somewhere between White Plains and Pleasantville, usually in daylight.

Anyway. The point of *this* story, and here I agree with Dr Poussard, is that by the time Olina resurfaced, I was ensconced, American-style, in a large suburban house, with an enormous, uniform stretch of green land all around it. One of Jimmy's uncles took care of the garden, which consisted mainly of a vast lawn and a small forest of gigantic evergreen trees which we sort of shared with invisible neighbours. Valhalla was, to my still-European eye, like a beautiful cemetery. People were never seen or heard in the streets – they were either quietly busy in their backyards or houses, or driving their cars around like armoured vehicles. I often wondered how large, warm families like Jimmy's had managed to change their habits so completely in the short time it had taken them to become middle-class suburban Americans, and move from the rich colour and warmth of Italian street life to the deadly monotony of these picture-perfect suburbs. But then, I had done exactly the same thing, only a little faster.

Olina had been a faithful correspondent throughout the years. She was much better at it than I was. Her letters were regular, long, detailed accounts (accompanied by many black and white photos) of her frenzied life, first as a drama student, then with her first husband, a television producer. She had merged, effortlessly, with the world my mother had once reigned in, but although she had always aspired to be a great actress, she never left the periphery. Olina played cute, kittenish roles, until her children were born, and lived in fear of losing her looks. Each pregnancy (there were two, three years apart) scared the hell out of her, but her biggest fear was the lonely role of full-time mother. I read her frantic reports and thought, you have no idea what loneliness is, you are surrounded by people, not lawns and trees, everywhere you look.

Her letters made me homesick, in a bittersweet sort of way, and helped me feel vaguely connected with Prague, year after year, even though it had long become an imaginary, unattainable mythical city in my mind. I thought I would never be allowed to go back there, to see it again with my own, adult eyes. But Olina was still living in her parents' apartment – both her grandmothers were dead. Sometimes she phoned me, usually on New Year's Eve, which was my birthday. She always sounded excited, in a manic sort of way, as if she had just been offered a major part in a big film. But her letters revealed how dissatisfied she was with her life, how deeply disappointed.

And I had so little to report myself – I was a housewife, sometimes efficient, sometimes slack. I also had two children, slightly older than Olina's, and I had never, ever had a professional career of any sort. It just didn't make sense to be Jimmy's wife and to have a job, so I never bothered. I read a lot, and ran a reading club in the local library, but that was it. I didn't worry too much about my slowly expanding waistline. I had little excuse to wear nice clothes, and Jimmy didn't care if I began to resemble his plump mother and his sisters. What could I tell her? She was jealous of my fairy-tale happiness, as she had been jealous of the kind of mother I had when we were children.

Dr Poussard asked me to gauge the frequency of Olina's phone calls in the last year or so. It's easy to remember that she started calling me more often after my thirty-fifth birthday. We talked about once a month, and suddenly there were joky hints about an affair she was having with an American businessman. She almost squealed with excitement one day when she told me she might have a chance to leave Czechoslovakia and go live in the US. I thought she was mad to talk like this over the phone, but she said, the revolution had changed everything, she was free to do and say what she wanted. 'But do you think it would be wrong to take the children away from their father?' she asked peevishly, and I was sure she was still joking.

A few months later, I had a jubilant – local – call from Olina's husband, Roman. He was in New York on business, and was ringing to give me his wife's love. Then he said, with a bit more colour in his slightly anaemic voice: 'You know, the revolution saved our marriage.' The explanation followed. Apparently, Olina had had an affair with an older American man – not her first one, it seems. She had spent most of the 1980s romanticizing the States and trying to practise her English with visiting tourists, academics and businessmen. But this time, he (Roman) stepped in, put an angry stop to the whole thing and it was now over. Life, he said softly, had been dreary until now, but was now exciting, due to the revolution. He kept repeating the word revolution, as if it could save him from all evil, and shield him from Olina's disappointment in him.

'Now,' he said, 'after all these years, there is real life in our Prague, and there will be no need for Olina to have these affairs with Americans. Things will go back to normal.' I didn't ask what he meant by 'normal'.

I didn't hear from Olina between that first call from Roman and his next one, from Prague. He was in tears. Olina left, with the kids, without any warning, while he was away on a weekend business trip in Germany. He came home and found that they were gone; there was a note on the kitchen table explaining where. She had gone to the States, with her latest lover ('a man named Jack Cohen, a fucking Jew,' he added). He kept crying, saying that he would probably never see them again, unless he could manage a trip to the US. He would wait for her; he wouldn't put her under pressure to come back until she was ready. He would try and think of their absence as a 'summer vacation'.

Jack Cohen, Roman had told me, lived not too far from me, in Armonk, New York. He was appealing to me to have some rational influence on his wife. He said I should try to convince her that, even though their marriage was basically non-existent, he was willing to accept anything she wanted. Non-existent, how? Well, they had no real family life. Olina would run out for entire nights as soon as he'd get back from work; she always wept after they made love.

Olina was to be my SUBURBAN NEIGHBOUR,

after all these years! I felt sorry for Roman, and for Olina, and for Jack Cohen, and most of all for the kids, but I also couldn't help finding the whole thing just a bit funny. I told Jimmy that I might hear from an old childhood friend of mine any day, and that she might need my help. He said, yeah, sure, OK.

A few days later, Olina finally called me, this time from Armonk. She was crying. Said she'd done a terrible thing, couldn't sleep at night, went to sleep with her daughter downstairs. Told me about Jack, revealing how carefully the 'elopement' had been planned by the two of them, months in advance. He had paid for everything. Then she told me how much she loved him, how much they loved each other. They simply had to be together because of their love. What an amazing lover he was, she had never experienced anything like it. We arranged that they would all come visit us on the weekend.

And I remembered that Roman had also told me something about Jack. They knew each other quite well. He had said that Jack had a weakness for Czech women and had finally 'settled' on Olina, telling her how wonderful she was and how wasted in Prague and in her hopeless marriage. And that he now wanted children (he was almost fifty, never married).

They came the following Sunday. It was very hot and I was suddenly drenched in nervous sweat when I watched Jack's car crawl up our long driveway. I had no idea what it would be like to be face to face with Olina, after all these years and in these strange circumstances. The last time I saw her, she was pointing her index finger at my mother's soiled green and orange paisley mini dress. Dr Poussard believes that I have always blamed Olina for making me lose my home.

And here she was, tall, slim, dressed in white, a bit tired around the eyes but otherwise still drop-dead gorgeous, helping a little blond boy and a little blonde girl out of the back of the car. And here was Jack Cohen, a mercurial man with a friendly smile and firm handshake.

Olina and I stared at each other for a few moments before we screamed and laughed hysterically. We must have hugged but I don't remember it. Her relief at seeing my heavy figure and my salt and pepper hair was clearly visible. But then she registered the house, Jimmy, my kids, and suddenly she lost her courage to compete with my happiness.

It was an awkward afternoon, but it could have been worse. The men did a barbecue, the kids sort of played, Olina and I talked and talked in the kitchen. No, it was Olina who did most of the talking. About Jack's unbelievable house in Usonia, a neighbourhood designed by Frank Lloyd Wright. 'It seems to grow out of the forest, as if it was put there by nature. The kids love it. Petr's eczema is almost gone. Prague is so polluted, you know!'

Of course, she sighed, the house is far from perfect. She has already told Jack they'll have to redo the kitchen, and move the bedrooms around so that the children can have a room each.

She was in mid-sentence when the phone rang. I was holding a platter full of French fries, so she answered it for me. It was Roman. He refused to talk to her, and hung up.

Then the tears came. Hers and mine. Olina's talent for melodrama had finally affected me, and I gave in to our mutual need to catch up with the lost years of our lives.

But Jimmy walked in and our brief moment of shared affection and supreme silliness was over.

Jimmy said: 'I'll drive over later with Jack and Olina, their kitchen plumbing needs looking at. Do you want to come? It might be cooler there than here.'

I didn't. I had had enough of Olina for one day, having established, in the course of that one afternoon, her amazing emotional neediness.

As it turned out, I didn't see much of her at all. At the end of the summer, Olina decided to go back to Prague, back to her husband. He promised to get her a job in television. She was disappointed, she said, by the unsophisticated American lifestyle, and hated Jack for giving her son a slap for misbehaving. Jack later told me that she had had unrealistic expectations about money, and had wanted him to spend unlimited amounts on the children. He also told me that she always cried after they made love.

But I knew there was another reason why Olina's love affair with America petered out. That hot Sunday, when Jimmy drove with them to Usonia in order to fix the antiquated plumbing in Jack's house, there had been a small incident. He was fiddling around with the hidden pipes in the kitchen and discovered that they were connected to other pipes he could not immediately identify, and found that they were clogged up. My conscientious husband then went upstairs, and found the source of the problem – a major blockage in an upstairs toilet. He could not understand how there could possibly have been a link between the toilet and the kitchen, but apparently some of these houses were a bit experimental, designed by students. Well, he unblocked the toilet, which caused a powerful jet of shit to cascade down those designer pipes straight into the kitchen sink, and beyond. Jimmy said that when he came downstairs, he found Olina sobbing, her white jeans and mini top dripping with ugly black and brown droplets. Jack Cohen tried to comfort her by saying that it was his fault, he forgot to warn her not to use that toilet. *He* certainly never did.

When Jimmy finished telling me this, I laughed so hard he thought I had lost my mind. Then I dialled my mother's number in Ottawa, but quickly hung up again. I decided to tell her this story face to face, and then, maybe, talk to her about going to Prague together. Just for a visit.

When I calmed down, I had to tell Jimmy that when they drove off, I was standing at the kitchen window, looking at the two almost identical-looking cars – Jack's and Jimmy's – moving in a straight line down the driveway. Everybody waved. I waved back. Then, and this is how I keep repeating it to Dr Poussard, and to Jimmy, because that is how it happened, I had a vision of the sky turning dark purple, almost black. I could almost feel the temperature drop suddenly and I heard what sounded like a fast train going right through my house. Then there was stillness again. The tornado had lifted both cars and dropped them, seemingly intact, on a distant neighbour's front lawn. My house was buried under God knows how many uprooted trees. Dr Poussard tells me to hang on to that image until I have learned the names of all those trees, in English.

Yoga Holiday

'Stand with your legs wide apart, hands on hips. Upper body very upright, straight back. Drop your shoulders, open your chest. Breathe in – and slowly lower your trunk, hands flat on the mat between your feet, if you can manage it. Press down. Brea-athe. Now look up, without shifting your position.'

I did and found myself staring and exhaling directly into a man's ass. Not a naked one, of course – this was a yoga class – but its trim shape was clearly outlined under the loose, cottony fabric of his red shorts. Somebody else was probably peering into my own not so trim behind. 'Please God don't make me fart' was the silent but powerful mantra going around the room. Someone's prayer went unheard.

Several taxing *asanas* later, we were asked to pair up with the nearest person and take turns in correcting one another's posture in a complicated twist. This was Day 1 of a week-long 'Yoga Holiday in Wales with Nina

Baldwin', a famous yoga teacher. Kneeling down and holding a complete stranger's sweaty legs was not a bad way to break the ice.

I looked to my left and saw a tall, elegant woman of about sixty. She smiled and offered to keep my feet on the ground while I tried to execute the twist according to Nina's instructions. 'Turn again with each exhalation. Look over your shoulder. Let your body follow your gaze, gently.'

Then it was my turn to help her. I clasped her surprisingly cool ankles, and as she rotated her supple waist, I kept my eyes on that interesting area behind her exposed knees which, more than her subtly lined face, brought back the memory of where we'd met before.

Twenty-five years ago, I had been her au pair. I was seventeen, a *lycéenne* from Paris, and she was 'Mrs Howard' to me. I was supposed to stay for a whole summer, but went home after three weeks, even though it meant spending all of August in a Communist Jewish camp near Lille. Mrs Howard was a bitch of cosmic proportions.

They lived in a secluded pseudo-posh estate somewhere in Croydon, at the end of a very neat row of three-storey townhouses. She had taught me to answer their phone 'Squirrel Hill 4733', and delighted in listening as I mangled the sound of those words with my accent. 'This is Nicole, our French au pair for the summer,' she said with a pleasant smile as she introduced me to a group of their dinner-party guests on my first evening there. 'She is quite dark, isn't she? Are you Jewish, Nicole?' No, of course not, I lied, and they all laughed.

I still don't know why I lied. I'd never done it before and never since. Maybe I already knew, instinctively, that Mrs Howard and I would not get along, and I did not want her to hate me *because I was Jewish*.

Now, her husband was quite a different story. When he picked me up from Waterloo Station in a huge, gleaming, white estate car, wearing white shorts and a white polo shirt, my teenage heart skipped a beat. Surrounded by all that whiteness on the way to Croydon, I couldn't help feeling *swarthy*. The tender blond hairs on his golden-brown arms and legs were practically reaching out for me, and I had a hard time focusing on answering his very friendly, polite questions. Mr Howard was lovely, kind and very shy. He spent most of the year working as an engineer somewhere in the Middle East, leaving his wife and two kids alone in Croydon – and me with them. Confession: had he been commuting to, say, the West End, I might have swallowed my pride and put up with Mrs Howard for the entire summer, if not longer.

The children, Julius, nine, and Anna, four, were very undemanding. Wise and charming Julius was my silent buddy. We watched TV together – we even cried over a mushy episode of *Emma*. Immensely sweet Anna tagged along and talked non-stop, completely ignoring the fact that I couldn't understand most of her baby English. I can honestly say that I fell in love with Mrs Howard's children, and had my responsibilities been restricted to looking after them, as the au pair agency had led me to believe, everything would have been fine.

But Lucy Howard had other ideas. I was to get up at six, before everyone else, and 'cook their breakfast', so that they could all wake up to the smell of frying bacon and eggs, toast and coffee. I was to 'do the whole house, top to bottom', every day. Help her with any cooking she was doing herself, clean the kitchen after each meal and spend time with the children before they went to bed. Occasionally, I would be asked to play with them in the neat garden, where Mrs Howard could always be seen, weather permitting, stretched out on a beach towel, trying to 'preserve her Spanish tan', as she put it. They had returned from a holiday not long ago.

I was a bookish teenager and had never cooked any-thing in my life, nor did I know what she meant by 'an English breakfast'. On my first morning, Charles Howard took it upon himself to teach me (his wife liked to sleep in a bit, he whispered apologetically). It seemed easy enough and, anyway, was a great excuse for spending a few moments alone with him. He was extremely skilful at tossing the bacon into the pan, turning it at just the right moment when it reached the perfect degree of shrinkage. Same with the eggs, usually at the same time.

After that first day, I was left to my own devices. And I screwed up royally, every single morning. In my hands, the bacon shrivelled into thin charcoal stripes. The eggs were always burned around the edges. The toast, ditto – and once it actually caught fire, causing Mr Howard to come racing down the stairs in a half-open dressing-gown. I felt like a character in a bad English sitcom. Following this disaster, I was no longer expected to prepare their breakfast.

Due to my nervousness and the mounting tension between us, I also started breaking their dishes, knocking down their china, clogging up their toilet. Once I slipped as I was coming down the stairs in my socks. I fell head down all the way like a drunk, ending up under a dainty little antique table at the bottom of the staircase. While I was squirming in pain, Lucy Howard arrived at my side, screaming: 'Oh my God, she broke it!' I remember Mr Howard staring at her in disbelief and saying, very softly, 'Darling, don't you think we ought to make sure the girl is all right?' He helped me to my feet and, later that evening, actually came to my room to see if I was OK. I was, but when I saw him I burst out crying – not telling him why, because it would have shocked the hell out of him. For a pampered girl from a nice, progressive French Jewish home, this had been quite a summer – I had experienced what it was like to be a servant, a foreigner, to have a sense of deep failure because I was terrible at the simplest household tasks, to completely forget that I was an intelligent human being with ideas and dreams of my own. The dislike I felt for Mrs Howard was also a new and powerful emotion – as was my crush on her *forbidden* husband.

So I just cried, and he put his arm around me and patted my head, and then he let his fingers play with my curls, and then he kissed me on the lips. I stopped crying and said, quite firmly as I recall, 'I think you'd better go now.'

'I go when I'm finished,' said the shy master of the house, just as firmly, and continued to be very nice to me until he heard his children's footsteps on the landing. The next morning, he was gone – back to Saudi Arabia.

The other erotic moment of my brief stay in Croydon was connected with Mrs Howard's sexy knees. One Sunday morning, out of sheer despair, I decided to phone an old friend of my father's, a writer living in Notting Hill. My father had told me to contact her if I needed anything, or if I wanted to stay in London overnight. When I dialled her number, a man answered, in a thick Slavic accent. My father's friend was away, he was her cousin, and was housesitting, as he had nowhere else to stay for the moment — he had recently escaped from Prague, and was also a writer — not a major one, he laughed. He knew my father as well, of course. Would I like him to come and visit me in Croydon? He was feeling old and depressed today, and if he could just spontaneously hop on a train in order to go see a very young girl whose voice he found enticing, it would make him feel better.

I was totally amazed by this conversation. I must have said yes. He arrived at lunchtime, a short, balding, middle-aged man with piercing blue eyes, messy eyebrows and a stream-of-consciousness, impassioned delivery. I introduced him to Mrs H and observed a stunning transformation in her demeanour. As soon as Karel Herman shot a wistful look in her direction and said, with a huge twinkle in his eye, 'I wish I could move to Croydon,' she relaxed her face into a softness I had never seen in her before, offered him tea and cake and chatted with such nonchalant flirtatiousness that I could only sigh and make a mental note to grow up and be more like her than like my own always well-behaved mother. (Although it did occur to me that, who knows, this Herman character may have the same effect on all middle-aged women!)

After tea, Karel Herman took me out for a walk before catching his train back to London. He gave me a long explanation of why he thought Mrs H was a very attractive woman. It was not her face, which he said was 'OK but nothing special'. Not her figure, either, which was 'excellent but not really exciting'. It was, he exclaimed with zest, that interesting area behind her knees which he had time to explore while she bent down in front of him to pour some tea. She was wearing shorts, and a lesser man might have derived more pleasure from the daring proximity of her derrière – as she had no doubt intended. But Karel Herman was a connoisseur of women, he could not be fooled. The back of Mrs H's knees spoke of warm, inviting crevices, of smooth skin and overall flexibility. It was, in short, like a quick glimpse of her vagina – here he stopped, looked directly into my eyes and asked: 'You *do* have a fully developed sex life, don't you?' I didn't, of course, but decided to make a move in that direction.

When I returned to the house, Mrs H was in high spirits, full of praise for my 'charming European guest'. There was a rare moment of genuine friendliness between us, which made it harder for me to tell her I would be leaving sooner than expected. In fact, tomorrow. Still, I think she was clearly relieved. As she seemed to be now, when the twisting exercise was over and we could each go back to our own mat. I knew we would have to reveal our identities sooner or later, but I wasn't going to rush it.

One problem with that resolution was that, on yoga

holidays, people tend to shed all their artificial skins by the time they've settled into their shared bedrooms. My roommate was standing by the Victorian sink, toothbrush in hand, when I came in and deposited my two heavy suitcases on the polished wooden floor. The bed I would have chosen for myself – at the far end of the enormous room, by the tapestried wall – was no longer free. I had to settle for the one near the door.

Julia was a leggy, willowy creature with a blazing mass of red hair and the proverbial alabaster skin. She looked like an ethereal Victorian ghost, perfectly at home in this secluded manor house which, as it turned out, she 'haunted' every night around eleven. Julia's nocturnal habit of swimming in the nude was soon the talk of our communal breakfasts and other gossipy sessions. Some of the hornier men – especially Sam, the athletic owner of the tiny red shorts – developed a bit of a problem with my roommate. He couldn't *not* join her in the pool, jacuzzi or sauna when he knew she was there, nor could he *not* swim naked so as not to look prudish next to her. But how, he whispered to me theatrically over organic porridge and dandelion coffeee one morning, how does one share all this aquatic space with her without getting a very rude, un-yogic erection? 'Try keeping your eyes on her *face*,' I suggested. 'Or you could talk to her about genetics – that's her field.'

Sam never solved his dilemma and continued to wallow in self-pity and self-imposed torture for the rest of the holiday. As Julia's roommate, I soon found out that he didn't have a prayer with her, and that there was a lovely little secret behind all that swimming and brushing of teeth. One of the less conspicuous men in our yoga class, a quiet computer technician from Manchester, was her lover. Both he and Julia were married with kids (she lived in London), and met only once a year on this yoga holiday. A barely noticeable sin, they felt, but one they could not be without. They disappeared, together, several times a day, no one knew where, and whenever they came back, Julia would spend a long time brushing her teeth.

Her boyfriend could not swim, but would sometimes sit in the jacuzzi or sauna and watch her being pursued and admired by Sam. She did it to drive him crazy, and it worked. I can't imagine what the rest of their year was like, back at home with their respective families. Probably perfectly ordinary.

Everybody had a story on this holiday, and exchanging them was a huge part of the fun we were having. My usual strategy of disguising myself as a boring French housewife living in London wasn't working this time, because the level of discourse was unusually high and frank. After one particularly stunning supper and several bottles of organic wine, we were all lolling around on the soft grass behind the conservatory, watching the teasingly slow sunset. I was asked and had to tell my own story.

I was from Paris, I said, but had come to live in England many years ago, because of a man. A very wealthy English Jew, a publisher. We met at the Frankfurt bookfair, where I was helping a French socialist publishing company with their stand. My socialism didn't prevent me from finding Hilary Dorfman's aggressive advances pretty exciting. I was only twenty, and he was a much older man, about forty, I thought (he was, in fact, fifty). His publishing company (expensively produced books on naval and military history) was not a very serious thing, more of a hobby for an energetic businessman who had time and money to spare. He was a huge man, very loud and jolly, and I liked him. I had just moved into his enormous, three-level flat in Kensington, after a quick honeymoon in Greece, when my brand new husband's age and previous medical history caught up with him and he dropped dead of a heart attack in the bathroom.

So here I was, a very wealthy young widow in London, calling myself Mrs Hilary Dorfman instead of Nicole Lazare – and still a socialist. I was now a proud owner of a ludicrous publishing company, and was 'related' to some of the 'best' Jewish families in town.

They were all anxious to meet me, and I endured it, for my dead husband's sake. But after a few years of this nonsense, I sold the company, made a few intentional social gaffes so as to give myself a bad name and stop the monstrously boring invitations from pouring in, moved to West Hampstead and became a rich rebel by joining and supporting every peace movement in town.

I had to explain to my yogic friends that by 'peace' I meant peace in the Middle East. I moved freely among Jewish and Arab groups, travelled to Israel and Egypt, Jordan and Morocco, meeting all sorts of luminaries (including a few kings), chatting them up and hoping that by liking this nice classy Jewish lady with a sexy French accent they will see the light and stop killing each other. Some people are frustrated writers – I was a frustrated diplomat.

I also had *very* interesting affairs with men who were as jolly and precariously unhealthy as my husband had been. Any average shrink could have told me that I was testing my powers as a murderess, trying to determine, on the basis of scientific evidence, whether it was I who had killed my husband. If I made it happen one more time, that hypothesis would have been confirmed.

Well, it never did happen, because I stopped myself, just in time, and became celibate.

'Very yogic,' whispered Julia's soft-spoken lover.

'Not yogic at all,' I said. 'Just totally fucked-up.'

We all laughed. The sun was finally down, and most people went inside.

One woman stayed behind, staring at me in disbelief. I knew who she was, and now she knew who I was, too. She smiled, looking incredibly young for her age. Karel Herman should see you now, I thought. And then I realized that he's probably dead, or very old.

'So you came back to England, Nicole. Why didn't you call us?'

'I didn't . . . I didn't think you'd like that. You hated me, didn't you? We hated each other. I thought you were a monster. But you seem pretty OK now, so maybe I was just a silly teenager.'

I hoped that would soften the blow, but Lucy Howard surprised me, once again.

'I *was* a monster, Nicole. Sorry. I think I was temporarily insane. I had a tiny excuse, though – Charles was in the process of leaving me. A French woman he met in Saudi Arabia was pregnant, and that was his last summer at home. So you see . . .'

We talked for hours. I suddenly had a glorious, corny feeling that life was nothing but kitsch, loads of it, and thank God for that.

'. . . what saved me from really losing it was meeting your friend, that Czech writer.'

'Herman?' I asked, incredulously.

'Yes, Karel. He suddenly reappeared at my door later that year, in the winter. Charles had already divorced me. Well. Karel was quite a man. He taught me a few things about myself.'

'I bet it had something to do with the back of your knees,' I laughed.

'What?' She didn't seem to know what I was talking about. Could it be that he had kept his deep insight into her sexuality to himself?

The following morning, Nina Baldwin decided to take us through some tough inverted *asanas*. We were to do handstands against the wall, helping each other to get our feet up and stay there for a few red-faced moments. Lucy and I were partners again. She was much better at it, and had a good, strong grip. While she held my legs as I tried not to lose my balance, standing on my hands, with my hair brushing the floor, she said, 'I always wondered why you denied that you were Jewish that time, when I asked you. *I* am, you know, and I knew you were as well – we had asked the agency to send us a Jewish au pair, if possible. That's why I was so mad at you and pretended I didn't care when you fell down those stairs. Anyway, I could see you were OK.'

'But . . . the bacon?' I croaked, as I returned to an upright position.

'Ah . . . Charles isn't Jewish, and I didn't care about those things. Still don't.'

At the end of each yoga class, you do the so-called corpse pose. Eyes closed, you just breathe, sink into the floor and let your body and mind feel heavy and empty. I could never achieve that total state of relaxation, there would always be some unpleasant nagging thought or emotion at the back of my mind or somewhere around my heart. For some reason, I was able to really let go that day, and feel light and, well, happy.

That night, Sam didn't go swimming. We had a discussion about my celibacy instead.

Peacocks

The strangest thing about this house is that the boiler is in the attic. Whenever the heating goes off, which happens quite often, Vera has to climb up the old aluminium ladder, squeeze through the narrow square opening in the floorboards and relight the pilot. The ladder is not very steady, and neither is Vera's hand when she pushes that button with her thumb and waits for the flame to grow bold, like a peacock's tail.

The last time she saw a real peacock was in the Moscow zoo. It wasn't that long ago but she can't believe it was really her, sitting on that bench in front of the rusty fence, sipping a lukewarm lemonade and reading through the letters she had received that morning from the agency. There were about five of them, from England, France and Germany. From men who wanted to marry a Russian woman, sight unseen. Well, not exactly, they all had her colour photo, but they could not know what she really looked like; couldn't see the big ugly birth mark, like a purple ink stain, on her right hip; couldn't feel the soft reddish down on her arms; couldn't taste the sweet and sour drops of sweat on her upper lip.

All five were offering her a more or less pleasant face, a more or less pleasant place to live. The agency took a hefty fee for matching up men and women who, for some reason, gave up on the idea of finding a partner closer to home. A friend had told Vera that Western men were afraid of Western women, and figured that Russian women were more pliable. That they would be happy with their new life, and wouldn't complain as long as it included a proper kitchen and a husband who didn't drink too much and wasn't violent. Apparently, Western men thought that to marry a Russian woman was to rescue her from a sinking ship.

Vera agreed, sort of. She had been desperate to leave Moscow, but not because she was in a precarious situation and felt the need to run away. Nor was she lonely. She had a decent job she almost loved, teaching English in a school for gifted children. She knew men who wanted her, and when she felt like it, she had fun with them. She might even have ended up marrying one of them, but one day she walked in on her parents while they were sitting on their old tattered couch in front of the television, holding bony hands like young lovers, immobile and glassy-eyed. She thought, with irritation, that if she gave one of them a little push they would both keel over, as if they were already lifeless. And she knew that they soon would be, and that she couldn't bear it. That evening, she looked up the address of Love Bonds Unlimited, a dating agency which specialized in bringing together 'young, responsible professionals from East and West'. All she had to do was write a letter, and send a decent photo of herself. They sent her some forms to fill in and sign, and took care of the rest. Some time later, she was given these letters, and asked to choose one of the men, if she could.

She chose Charles not because he looked or 'sounded' better than the others, but because he lived in London. His letters were restrained, didn't say too much, his photographed smile seemed relaxed and unexciting. But his address was sexy – Kensington Gate. The first word reminded her of Diana's funeral, the palace, all those flowers. Vera had been impressed by so much grief – there was nobody in her own country she could imagine causing such a flood of tears. And the second word – Gate – was a curious mystery: how could a street be called 'gate'? It implied grandeur, largesse, maybe a palace or at least a Victorian mansion. Lords and ladies, feasts and parties, butlers and servants in uniform. Vera decided that she would be kind to her servants, and answered Charles's letter in her best handwriting.

After several such letters, they agreed to forgo the preliminary meeting the agency recommended, and to take a chance on each other. Vera arrived at Heathrow on a warm, sunny October day. Charles was holding up a bright yellow sign with her name written on it, in Russian. She saw him first. He was shorter than she had imagined, and rounder too. In fact, he was definitely a bit fat, but Vera would take care of that. He looked younger than his thirty-six years, in spite of the candid baldness and his serious, bespectacled look. But Vera didn't dislike him at all, and approached him with an open smile, as if they were old friends.

To Charles, Vera was a kinky dream come true. He had asked her to wear boots and a miniskirt for the flight, so that he could recognize her instantly and walk away if there was anything distasteful about her appearance. But there wasn't; she was slim, petite, everything in the right place. She let her heavy blonde hair cascade down her shoulders, to impress him as much as possible as fast as possible – and it worked. Even though her clothes were not quite up to scratch, Charles was pleased. And when he heard the funny Russian accent in her otherwise excellent English, he almost gasped with excitement.

Vera remembers the shyness of those first moments, the yellow roses he had brought to the airport. She had to refuse them – didn't he know that yellow roses meant heartache, separation? 'That's just your bloody Russian superstition,' he snorted, but dutifully turned around and handed the rich bouquet to a surprised old lady. Vera had laughed, and Charles had registered the throaty quality of her laugh. Everything was coming together nicely.

As they drove home, Vera had looked at the grey suburbs, wondering whether *this* was London. When they entered inner city traffic, she followed the taller buildings with her eyes and waited, patiently, for Kensington Gate to emerge. Finally, it did, and her joy at seeing the dignified elegance of the building Charles referred to as 'theirs' was uncontrollable. She wanted to scream with delight, but squeezed his hand instead.

Then it began to sink in that they were entering the big house through a small side door, and that Charles did not have the key to it. They were let in by a large dark woman, who smiled warmly at Vera but not at Charles. Going up a narrow staircase, all the way to the top floor, Vera panted: 'This is *your* house?' with an unintended stress on the word 'your'. Charles unlocked a door at the top of the stairs, and they were in a small attic room, with a sink in the corner and a shower behind a transparent plastic curtain. There was a bed, a desk, two chairs. A wardrobe. A small fridge. A kettle. That was it. Everything was neat and clean, but there was absolutely no room to move. And it was hot.

Of course, Vera cried when Charles told her that he was only a butler in this nice Kensington mansion. Of course, she forgave him when he confessed that he hadn't said so in his letters because he was afraid she would not take him seriously. She would stay anyway, she said. They would manage. Having come this far, she didn't think she could ever go back to Moscow, even though right now that was what she really wanted to do. That first night, Charles gave her the bed and spent the night on a futon mattress on the floor.

Charles was too insolent to be a successful butler. His employer was a famous heavy metal rock star called Wild Bobby Blunder; the house was one of his many homes. Wild Bobby had a reasonably pretty, bulimic wife, Carol, who wrote all of his effusive lyrics and ran the households – all of them – like an experienced Victorian aristocrat. Which is exactly what she was, give or take a hundred years.

The Blunders had servants, maids, cooks, nannies, secretaries. Carol kept detailed files on all her staff, including secret facts about their intimate habits and inclinations, everything she could find out about them. She controlled a small empire of nice people who were enslaved to her for the greater glory of working for the protean lead singer of the Red Trouts and his small family. Carol was moody, capricious, even cruel, but never impolite. Her 'please' and 'thank you's were thin icicles permanently suspended in mid-air, like frozen rain.

Charles didn't remember why he had become a butler, of all things. Vera had tried to make him explain, but it was useless. Couldn't he have studied something, learned a trade, couldn't he have acquired anything but this strange skill of serving rich people? Didn't he feel humiliated, dehumanized? Charles smiled and reminded Vera that had he been the owner of this vast residence and not the butler, she would have been quite happy with her lot. Vera accepted this gentle criticism of her without putting up too much of a fight. She was similarly receptive to Charles's first, very tentative embrace. Shortly after her arrival in London, they were married, as planned. It was a civil wedding. Charles's parents were dead, and his two brothers lived in Australia. So only a handful of his friends joined them for a small celebration in a pub afterwards. The Blunders gave them two return tickets to Calais as a wedding gift.

Charles had become a major thorn in Carol's side, long before Vera arrived on the scene. He had been Bobby's butler for almost a decade. What Carol knew but chose to ignore was the fact that Bobby and Charles were of exactly the same age, and had once been schoolmates, and friends, in a posh boarding school. Charles used to fold Bobby's shirts even then, and pack his suitcase for him before each holiday visit home. They had always kept in touch, and when Bobby became rich and notorious he offered his old mate the butler's job. This had made Charles more happy than grateful.

His manner toward Bobby's wife was anything but deferential. He was not beyond informing her that 'her breath needed freshening', or that her new designer haircut made her look 'like a vampire on steroids'. Once, when she was about to step out to go to a charity gala event, dressed to kill in a tight gold-green number and matching stilettos, Charles commented, drily, that her nipples were protruding several significant inches *below* the intended height, and offered to run out and get her one of those magic, invisible bras.

But Wild Bobby Blunder needed Charles. In the unstable world of fame-induced, drug-infested madness, Charles was, for Bobby, an oasis of calm and practical wisdom. He had a way with clothes, with the telephone, with food and drink, even with drugs, that made Bobby feel organized and normal, connected with the real world. He adored Charles's sardonic comments, especially those directed at Carol. If it had been in Bobby's power to sack Carol and keep Charles, he would probably have done so, and what a trip *that* would be . . .

As it happened, Carol got her wish first, using Vera as an excuse. She bribed a private investigator to research the 'real' story behind Love Bonds Unlimited, and 'discovered' a clandestine international connection between the dating agency and the Russian mafia. This was enough to persuade Bobby that Charles had to go; they could not possibly risk their safety, and that of their children, by allowing Charles to continue as their employee. He was asked to leave, with three weeks' notice.

They used the time to rent a small house in a quiet, green suburb called Cockfosters, at the northern end of the Piccadilly line. Charles's savings were just about enough for some basic furniture and an Ikea kitchen Vera could photograph for her parents in Moscow, as proof of the material success of her match. Then came the big question: what now?

Charles's attempts to find work as a butler were a complete failure. Carol's lukewarm letter of recommendation made sure that he wasn't granted too many interviews; and when he did get them, his lofty airs and laconic answers to his prospective employers' questions quickly destroyed every chance he had of becoming someone else's butler. And what else could he do? He tried applying for jobs as a chef, but ran up against similar problems. After two months of living on his savings, Charles gave up his fruitless job hunting and started collecting his unemployment benefit.

Vera was at a loss. She couldn't teach English in

London, with her Russian accent. She could, conceivably, teach Russian, but the idea of teaching adults made her shy. She was too restless to be a housewife, and anyway, she couldn't afford it. She had little hope of becoming pregnant, after her seven abortions – that popular form of Soviet birth control. There had been complications and doctors told her not to expect miracles. Charles knew and didn't seem to mind. In his phlegmatic state, he didn't seem to care about anything at all.

There was a great deal he could have done every day to make their house more liveable. He could have painted the rooms, replaced some cracked tiles in the bathroom, adjusted the front door so that it wouldn't shut with a bang. He could even, as Vera had suggested, get someone to move the temperamental boiler from the attic to the kitchen, to save Vera all this climbing.

But Charles had become a disinterested observer in his own home. He paid attention to two things only: his and Vera's clothes, which he kept neatly folded and meticulously clean and ironed, and their food. He prepared small, colourful feasts, several times a day, and grew fatter and fatter. Far from being in control of her plump husband's diet, as she had originally planned, Vera was becoming chubby herself. Her new English clothes did not fit her.

During her first London winter, they spent long, slow

days in their house, eating, watching television, drinking, smoking joints. Their sex life was exceedingly boring – even Vera knew that. Charles didn't want much of anything except good food. On New Year's Eve, there was a phone call from Bobby, wishing 'him and his lovely Russian lady a happy New Year'. This brought a bit of colour to Charles's pudgy cheeks, but only for a moment. It was a short call.

One day, Vera discovered that she had developed a hobby. She was spending many hours each day studying the London A-Z. She started with a small, ring-bound one, and when it fell apart she moved on to a very large one, in a heavy hard cover. She read, studied and memorized the names of all the streets, avenues, roads, crescents, parks. Occasionally, she would ask Charles to help her pronounce a name correctly, but not too often. She had developed a feel for the city, if only on paper.

This was soon followed up by the real thing. She would buy a travel card, and explore every corner of London, meticulously, day by day. Soon she knew every tube stop on every line, most of the bus routes, neighbourhoods in every part of the city. She was no longer a tourist; she had become a passionate Londoner, and by the time spring came she knew the city by heart. The strange thing was that when a street with what she thought was a romantic English name turned out to be a grimy slum, she was not disappointed. She talked to people everywhere, men, women, children. Some men thought she was a prostitute, but when she stopped wearing her provocative clothes and learned to live in her worn jeans, they stopped making passes at her.

She liked some neighbourhoods better than others. Most of all, she liked Camden, because it was nothing like the regal London she had imagined, and because she felt invisible there. A white note in a window in Camden High Street caught her eye – 'Lady Cab Driver Required. No Experience Necessary.' She applied, but immediately faced a problem: she didn't own a car, which was a condition for getting the job. Charles had had to sell his old Ford Escort, to pay the rent.

That night, Vera gave Charles a hard time. She hadn't been demanding so far, but she felt entitled to some effort on his part to make things work. Couldn't he buy a car? No, he couldn't. How about taking out a loan? He had no steady income, and couldn't repay it. But she would be earning money by driving the cab! They could not rely on that.

'You useless English bastard,' Vera said. Then she picked up a large platter, which Charles had just arranged beautifully with his latest creation – a Thai green fish curry, surrounded by delicate lime leaves and rice – and smashed it with all her might in the kitchen sink. The green stuff was splattered all over the sticky counter, on Charles's shiny forehead, on the grubby kitchen floor.

She thought he was going to hit her when he made a small step in her direction, but Charles never hit anybody in his life, not even Bobby when he had ridiculed his dedicated but talentless trumpet playing in school. 'Save your filthy breath for blow jobs,' he had said to Charles, in front of a chosen gang of popular boys, who then proceeded to demand just that. Wild Bobby Blunder remembered, and was a frequent visitor in Charles's stuffy attic room – until Vera's advent there.

Now, Charles reached for the phone behind Vera's blonde head, and dialled the Blunders' main London number. His voice was a little less measured than usual when he asked for Bobby, saying it was urgent. Vera heard the singer's loud screech when Charles asked him for a car. After what sounded like a great deal of pleading on the other end, Charles hung up, satisfied.

The following morning, Bobby's chauffeur delivered a five-year-old black Vauxhall Cavalier that used to belong to one of the Blunders' servants. Charles and Vera were allowed to keep it. It was a gift.

Vera became a London minicab driver. She was in demand – most of the company's female customers asked for her by her cab number – zero seven – and many male ones as well. She was able to put her near-perfect knowledge of London geography to good use, and loved it. But she was also living dangerously, criss-crossing the deserted streets alone at night, heading in all directions to pick up unknown passengers.

Because she wasn't driving a black taxi, there was no partition between her and the back seat. Anything could go on there, anything could happen. Vera learned to control her own safety by anticipating trouble, by driving away without her fare if the person looked suspicious or unsavoury. It didn't always work.

Once, she picked up a bona fide rapist. She knew he was a rapist because he told her so, with his hand groping for her breast under her seatbelt. It was two in the afternoon, bright grey London daylight. Somewhere in Kentish Town. Vera hit the brakes, bringing a long line of impatiently hooting cars to a halt, turned around and slapped the man's ugly face. Actually, it wasn't ugly at all. She remembers that he had delicate English features, and smelled of expensive aftershave. The smell lingered long after the man bolted from her car.

To Vera's surprise, Charles didn't seem too concerned about her. 'Just look after yourself and you'll be fine,' he'd said when she drove straight home, shakily, after that encounter. He couldn't imagine what they would do without her income. His recipes were becoming more and more elaborate, as Vera's money could pay for more expensive, rare ingredients. But cooking was still the only focus of Charles's solitary life. His working days seemed to be over.

So she continued to cruise the streets of London in her black Vauxhall. Once, she drove an elegant Russian couple, tourists from Moscow, on a shopping spree. She didn't let on that she understood them and eavesdropped on their quarrel about how many presents they still had to buy for their parents, and whose parents deserved the more costly gifts. The wife seemed to have the upper hand in the argument, as her parents were looking after the couple's children, whereas his were 'parasites', she spat out, 'blood-sucking parasites'.

Vera dropped them off in Bond Street, and thought of her own parents as she headed back to Camden. She sent them regular parcels with lovely things, warm clothes, even money, but she knew that what they really wanted was to have her back. She parked the car in the first available empty space, took the key out of the ignition, and wept.

And now, here she was, hypnotized by the blue flame of the pilot light, which had flared out to its maximum width and height. The bloody boiler was humming extra loudly, which meant that Charles was now running a bath, with one of his many luxurious bath salts. Gianni Versace was his favourite. He loved Versace Homme perfume, and always wanted to smell the feminine Versace version on Vera. Not that it led to much more than an occasional sweet cuddle after a superb dinner. So what sort of life *was* this, Vera wanted to scream as she climbed down the ladder.

The bathroom door was closed, and Vera never disturbed Charles during his nightly ritual. But tonight, she was feeling especially lonely. She pressed the handle, noiselessly. There was her English husband, submerged under a solid mountain of perfumed bubbles. His steamed-up glasses were staring at her from the cracked window sill. Charles was half-blind without them, she knew. But surely not too blind to see his own erection growing firmly out of the water, nor too vain to admire its imposing majesty.

Vera closed the door as quietly as she had opened it, tiptoed into the kitchen and burst out laughing. The sad joke was that she had never seen this much of Charles before.

She asked her cab company if she could work tonight, even though it was late and she hadn't planned on it. She was lucky: within minutes, she was in her car and on her way to pick up a passenger from a Highgate pub, a woman. A Mrs Baker, going to Knightsbridge.

Mrs Baker turned out to be Carol Blunder, using her real name. She didn't recognize Vera, barked her Kensington Gate address as politely as her drunken state allowed it, and promptly fell asleep in the back seat.

Vera studied Carol's features in the mirror, whenever they stopped near a street lamp. She had a small, pinched face tonight, like one of those shrunken heads she once saw in an anthropology atlas. Her skin was very white, with large red blotches. Suddenly, Vera's own secret birthmark didn't look bad by comparison.

She drove smoothly, expertly, wondering why Carol didn't have her own driver with her. When she pulled up in front of the house, at three in the morning, Carol was still fast asleep. The house was dark.

Vera turned off the motor and got out. This one's on me, she decided, and lifted the featherlight Carol out of the back seat. She had just managed to prop her up against the heavy door, when it opened and there was Wild Bobby in the same silk pyjamas Charles wore (he had once ordered several dozen of them and gave a few to his butler), bleary eyed but sober. He recognized Vera instantly. In fact, he recognized her before he recognized his own wife. He didn't really know about Carol's drinking; she usually managed to do it when he couldn't see the results.

Together, they carried Carol inside and put her gently down on an enormous leather couch. Vera explained the situation. Bobby reached for his money, but couldn't find any. Carol's bag had nothing in it except an electronic organizer. She was in an alcoholic stupor, out cold. There were no servants in the house, no one to ask for the cash.

Bobby offered to write a cheque, but Vera said it didn't matter, and got up to go. Bobby said she didn't have to go yet. She said she did. No, sit. Tell me about Charles. How is he? I miss him, you know. And his washed-out eyes said to her, right now, you can be Charles. *Be* Charles.

What Western men don't know about Eastern women is that they are unafraid to trust their instincts. There was violence in Bobby that night, but Vera said, I might as well tell you. Carol was right about the Russian mafia, but she didn't know the full scale of it. Charles and I are in charge of some pretty big show-business accounts. You're one of them. That's why I drive around at night. Collecting. Carol has been taking care of it. She promised us a hundred grand, but look at her. So Bobby, write the cheque. Please? That should do it for the next ten years or so. Who knows, we might even leave you alone. Otherwise, those guys are ruthless. Did you know that one of your nannies has been corresponding with an Uzbeki man through Love Bonds Unlimited?

Carol stirred, moaned, didn't wake up. Wild Bobby Blunder, the amorphous idol of an inchoate teenage crowd, groaned, broke out in a cold sweat and wrote the cheque. A small dent in one of his bank accounts.

Vera drove back through the mauve shimmer of an early July sunrise, slowly, leisurely. She had unlawfully blackmailed the man who had stolen her husband's dignity. No matter. She would encourage Charles to write a cookbook, and the boiler will finally leave the attic.

Framed

'If you're converting to please your precious Max, you're wasting your time. He's not even circumcised,' said Daniel Zohar. He was talking to his own reflection in the mirror, trying to gauge, and improve, the emotional intensity of his own voice – a dull instrument. He should not sound, or look, too involved, nor too cool. Just right.

He could do with a bit more finetuning, but this had been a successful rehearsal – and hopefully the final one. He felt ready to deliver these lines in front of his intended audience – Monika – who should be arriving any minute for her Hebrew lesson. He was her teacher, preparing her for the conversion. But what he really wanted was to reveal to her that she was sold on the idea of marrying a devil, a cynical German Jew who was practically a goy, and that he, Daniel, loved her more than a guy like Max Kamenski ever could. He was ready to tell her, but he had felt ready before, and failed. The part of him that still prayed, occasionally, with honest fervour, begged God that today he would manage to say those words to her. Or something. Time was running out – this was to be her last lesson before her trip to New York, where she had registered to undergo an orthodox conversion under the supervision of not one but three illustrious rabbis. Daniel had a recurring dream – a nightmare! – about the divine Monika *splashing about in the* mikveh *with three naked bearded men.* His own role in the dream was unclear – he was trying to save her, as if from a drowning, but at the same time he felt obliged to join in their laughter, and immerse himself in the ritual bath. The dream always left an echo in his head.

He adjusted his knitted wine-red kippa, pushing it a little more towards the back of his head, a little more out of sight. He checked his watch: she was five minutes late. This was unusual. Monika was always on time. Her exercise books were impeccably neat, her Hebrew handwriting almost flawless. Strangely, her German handwriting was not neat at all. She penned large, fat, scrawly letters, barely legible.

Daniel decided that today he looked almost good enough to convince her that they would make an attractive couple. It was true that she was a tiny bit taller than him, but his big black curls made up for the missing inches. It was also true that Max was taller than Monika, in spite of his ridiculous bald head, but what did that mean? Daniel was younger, his body was a feast of muscular power, his face ... He couldn't really judge, but it seemed to him that women tended to smile at him a lot, that they liked to run their fingers along his broad jaw, to kiss him without holding back. German women loved his long eyelashes, and Daniel wasn't surprised; German men had naked eyes, flat faces, lips that looked unyielding. Maybe that was the reason why his star pupil had fallen for Max, whose lips were full and elastic, curving up or down into smiles or sneers like a pair of short, fat snakes. Daniel will break it to her that there is no point in her becoming Jewish for an arrogant, cynical intellectual like Max, who is not sure of anything at all, least of all his feelings for a woman.

Monika will notice that he's dressed better than usual today. Daniel has decided to imitate Max's style, which is relaxed but not careless. She obviously likes that, and would never go out with a man who is clad like an Israeli macho import. Even if Daniel can't help being one – at least he doesn't have to look it. The tell-tale signs of being an Israeli paratrooper out of uniform were hard to hide, but Daniel was also a graduate student in German history, finishing his doctorate at the University of Hamburg. A robust, healthy Middle Eastern man in a

European shell. Why should that be any less attractive to Monika than Max's watered-down version of a central European Jew, with his plaintive voice and drooping eyelids?

He was considering brushing his teeth one more time when the doorbell rang, at last. Daniel opened his door to a teary-eyed Monika. She stood there, clutching her bag like a schoolgirl. Suddenly, she seemed much smaller than him. He touched her arm and she collapsed on his shoulder, sobbing for some reason which he did not yet know. When she told him, his prepared speech came naturally, as if he had not rehearsed it a million times.

Monika Mitgang's story was simple. She came across Max Kamenski's first novel in the Hamburg bookstore where she worked, and its pungency took her breath away. Max's novel was like a stark cityscape populated by Jews, Germans, Israelis, East Europeans, Americans – all disingenuous, villainous, deceitful, faithless. They spoke acerbic lines, did unspeakable things to each other and seemed to have been created by an author who did not love them. Yet Monika felt that he did love them, and when she met him at a booksigning evening, she told him so.

Max was amused, but did not invite her to meet him sometime, somewhere. She looked, to him, like all his women – blonde, sleek, striking, long-legged, young blue eyes full of blind adoration for his sharp statements about Jews and Germans. He knew, instantly, that she would be the kind of woman who would laugh at his asinine jokes, but would never actually *make* a joke herself. She would arrange her life around his needs, and find it exciting. They would have great sex, but within, say, six months, boredom would set in. Guilt and/or duty would prevail for another six months, and then he would have to cut her off from his life like a piece of gum that had become entangled in his hair. Not that he had any hair to support this image, but it worked.

They finally met, for real, under very unexpected circumstances. Max was not only a writer. He also dabbled in photography. For his latest series of nude torsos framed by large ornamental windows, Max needed models. Monika saw the whimsical ad in the local paper, and recognized it as a quote from Max's novel. It said: 'Required: tall female model to fill a window, by amateur photographer.'

When she phoned him, Max was very impressed that Monika had identified the quote; in his novel, *Framed*, a lecherous Jewish painter in Weimar Berlin advertises for a female model in exactly the same words. He hired her, of course. He would have done so in any case: Monika's body was built to be celebrated in any visual artform. She was silent while he was taking the pictures, but talked a blue streak afterwards, in bed. Then she was silent again, when they went out to eat at a Turkish restaurant near his house, and resumed her chatty mode in her own apartment, where they finished that long first day, and night.

Max discovered that he had a huge appetite for Monika's conversation, and for her silences. Being with her did not feel wrong at all, or fortuitous, or calculated. He felt lucky when she held him, he felt happy when they were together, alone or with others. Monika told him it was love, and he believed her.

What he didn't believe was that this meant they had to plan any sort of future. Max didn't think about the future because it frightened him. The only thing that frightened him even more was the past. He was thirty-six and had spent most of his thinking life trying to decipher the meaning of things that happened long before he was born. This approach left no room for assuming responsibility for what would happen in the course of the as yet unlived part of his life.

It took Monika four years to fully grasp the real depth of Max's neurosis. For example, every morning at seven, Max had to flee, Cinderella-like, from the presence of even the most desirable human beings back into his apartment, in order to be able to work; and if Monika was staying the night, she would be woken up by him at seven, gently, and sent home in a taxi. The idea of sharing a leisurely breakfast together, or, God forbid, wasting a whole morning without trying to write, was anathema to Max. Not that he was a very prolific writer. He laboured over his manuscripts like an old Jewish scribe, huffing and puffing and tearing them to pieces. His novel was a slim volume, about two hundred pages. It had taken him nine years to write it.

The conversion had not been Max's idea. Monika announced it one day, as a decision she had taken, not as something she wanted to discuss. She had been to see Rabbi Krauthammer, she said to Max.

'And?'

'And . . . he'll advise me but he won't do the conversion. He said you . . .'

Max was suddenly interested. One of the minor heroes in *Framed* was a Polish rabbi who returns to Germany after the war and looks after the elderly invalid mother of one of his Nazi jailers. Max had borrowed Krauthammer's characteristics (thin, fragile frame, heavy red beard, a heavy accent which ignored the umlaut in German), though not his personal history.

Krauthammer's story was different. He had spent the war in America, not in Auschwitz, and could not wait to return to Europe when it was over. He would have gone back to Poland had he not been greeted with a post-

Holocaust pogrom in Kielce, his home town. An old friend invited him to Hamburg, where he gradually became the small head of a small rudderless community. Max was most definitely, and demonstratively, *not* a member of Krauthammer's clan, in spite of being the most notorious young Jew in Germany. So what did the Rebbe say to Monika about Max?

'He said you should come to synagogue with me every *shabbat*. He said you should learn Hebrew, and study everything I study, so that we can have a proper Jewish . . .'

She stopped. She hadn't meant to say this much. Max would explode.

But he hadn't. He just laughed, as if Krauthammer had made a very good joke. And, seeing the worried expression on Monika's face, he agreed to join her for some Hebrew classes with young Daniel Zohar.

Max had attended exactly two of those classes — enough to see, with what he called his 'writer's sixth sense', the emerging story line: Daniel would end up falling in love with Monika, and, sooner or later, he would try to seduce her with his smug, infantile, Israeli competitiveness. But instead of trying to block this development, by, say, convincing Monika to find another Hebrew teacher, he withdrew entirely. He let Monika decide for herself.

This was two years ago. In that time, Monika saw Daniel once a week. Max was right: Daniel was visibly, obsessively in love with her. If she cancelled a class because she wasn't feeling well, he would come to see her, bringing a Hebrew tape and flowers. Whenever she mentioned Max's name, casually, his face would contort a tiny bit and he would say something *very nice* about him: Max is an excellent writer, he should be more famous. Or, after they had all gone swimming: Max must have had quite a head of hair, judging by his chest and back. Or: Max is trying so hard to be a *Jewish* writer; pity he didn't stay in the class, he could have learned more Hebrew and maybe, who knows, gone to live in Israel.

This last line had been a favourite of Daniel's until it hit him that he would be returning to Israel himself very soon. He had spent several years in Hamburg, dividing his time between research for his thesis on Martin Luther and helping with a few security assignments he could not discuss – not even with Monika, who had become a close friend, if nothing else. Until today . . .

She was actually *sobbing into his pecs*, whimpering something about Max and New York and Krauthammer. Daniel was in heaven. Not because she was unhappy, but because she was confiding in *him*.

'It's off,' she wailed, 'Max isn't coming with me. And it's Kraut . . . Krauthammer's fault.'

Daniel was confused. What's off? The conversion? The wedding? As far as he knew, it hadn't even been discussed.

Monika wiped her wet nose on the back of her hand, which she buried inside his sweater – very, very near his heart, which was going wild.

She took a deep breath. Max, she explained, was refusing to come to New York with her, as they had planned, because Rabbi Krauthammer told Max that he would ban him from his synagogue, and would even try to have him excommunicated, à la Spinoza.

Why?

Because of Max's article in *Sieben Tage* magazine. Hadn't Daniel read it?

Apparently, Max had delivered another one of his eloquent salvos against both Jews and Germans, but this time he had gone too far. Even Monika thought so. He had written that a prominent Hamburg rabbi was involved in frequenting certain establishments on the Reeperbahn which were known for their Israeli prostitutes. Max's piece was laudatory, not critical. He praised the rabbi for his realistic understanding of human needs, and for his original and liberal approach to the Zionist cause. According to Max, the rabbi in question was merely interested in looking after the welfare of these young expatriate Israelis, and in helping them return home when they were ready. His criticism and wrath fell on the German government, for refusing to grant the women political refugee status (many of them were Russian immigrants to Israel who had been categorized as non-Jewish by the Israeli religious establishment, and could not even be buried there), and on the women themselves, for refusing to learn German and accept German customers.

Daniel was confused. Where, exactly, was the problem?

Monika sat up a little, without removing her hand from the warm crevice near his armpit.

'Don't you get it? Max is pissed off because, a., he is not acceptable to these whores, and for some reason he wants to be. They think he's a real German. And b., Krauthammer's attack on him is the final straw. Now he doesn't want to be Jewish at all. He's throwing a tantrum. And I've had it with his infantile selfishness, his idiotic habits, all his fucking Jewish shit—'

She jumped up suddenly, leaving a cold spot where her hand had been. Her voice, about to deliver a desperate assault on Max, retreated from a near-hysterical pitch with impressive self-control. She realized that she had been talking to Daniel without really seeing him, as she had always done. But now he could not be overlooked as he took both her hands, pulled her firmly back to the sofa and said, calmly:

'If you're converting to please your precious Max, you're wasting your time. He's not even circumcised.' And, after a pause: 'Forget New York. Forget Max. Come to Israel with me. You'll convert there, it's dead easy, and we'll get married. That's easy too, if you love me just a little.'

Daniel wouldn't have mumbled that last sentence if he hadn't remembered a thousand moments in the past when Monika seemed so much more at ease with him than with Max. Now, he waited for her verdict. He needn't have worried; Max had already foreseen this particular scene, and had informed Monika, before she stormed out of his apartment earlier that morning, that, as she was obviously a German self-hater and needed to be screwed by a Jew, Daniel would do just fine. Then, in a softer tone: 'Sorry. Didn't mean that. But I think he is nuts about you. Give the guy a chance.' So she did, and it didn't feel bad at all. Daniel's trimmed penis made her feel like a proper Jewish bride, which she was soon to become. And he surprised her, pleasantly, by having a highly developed post-coital sense of humour. Monika loved his fantasy of her swimming in the *mikveh* with a bunch of rabbis, and loved him for not including himself in it. Max would have put his mocking persona right at the centre of such a scene. He would be mooning the rabbis, then taunting them with his uncircumcised (but oh so grand) dick. To hell with him. She was going to Israel.

2

She stood naked behind the cracked wooden blind, unseen, alone. She had let the house deteriorate in Daniel's absence, had allowed dust and sand to creep in and settle on everything, had not shut windows during sandstorms. She wished she could feel a cooling layer of salty sweat between her skin and the grimy glass of the balcony window, but everything felt burning hot to the touch, even glass, even wood. Hot and dry, not hot and wet.

Through the free spaces between the chipped slats, she saw the monotonous landscape of flat, sooty white roofs and television antennas. Cylinder-shaped solar heaters behind shiny angular shields and round satellite dishes interrupted the sleepy tedium. She wished she could at least smell the sea from where she stood, but this wasn't Tel Aviv, where she had wanted to be. This was Beer Sheva, where they had to move because of Daniel's job at the university. This was the desert, and she hated it.

Their first year in Israel had been a slice of Mediterranean heaven. The wedding had quickly become a blurred memory of a satiny affair at which she felt both celebrated and very, very foreign. They rented a tiny apartment off Dizengoff, five minutes from the beach, where she was free to waste her days while Daniel continued to work on his thesis. She had brought her savings with her, and did not want to do anything except wallow in the red heat and the stark light of her new home, soaking in the sunshine and the flirtatious attentions of many Daniel-lookalikes.

Monika did not flirt back, but did enjoy her newly found sense of being appreciated, in a rough and direct way, for her beaming looks. All these dark, smiley, coarse guys seemed to want her, and she didn't mind – as long as they stayed a safe distance away from her beach towel. She stretched her long limbs this way and that, caressed her willing body under the guise of applying suntan lotion, turned the baby pink palms of her hands upwards to show off the contrast with her bronze skin. She looked, she knew, like a Scandinavian tourist, and loved it when the natives tried their funny English on her ('You like Israeli bitch?') – and she answered back in fluent, only slightly accented Hebrew: 'Ata mastir li et hashemesh.' (You're blocking the sun.)

Once in a while, Daniel would take a break from his writing and join her. He liked to surprise her by throwing hot sand, gently, against the rosy soles of her feet, until she became aware of his presence and sat up. The tough regulars would look at Daniel with envy, when they saw Monika's undisguised affection. Pretty soon, she established her status on the beach as an untouchable foreign beauty with a mysteriously perfect command of Hebrew, and an authentic Israeli husband. From time to time she met German tourists. She listened to their familiar voices, especially Northern ones, and felt homesick for the uncomplicated life she could have had if she had never met Max. But when they tried to claim her as one of their own, she felt distant, as if she had never known the grey, efficient precision of her home town, and was a native of this chaotic, aggressive, messy, burning Middle East.

She spent mornings and afternoons by the sea, hot lunchtime siestas and nights at home. Daniel was always ready for her, as if the years of loving her against her love for Max had built up in him an endless supply of desire. Monika was not a reluctant lover, but they both knew that their marriage lacked an edge, was too serene, unruffled. Just a tiny bit of anger, uncertainty or even hate was needed to disturb that perfect balance. Monika's devotion to Daniel was a tender friendship; his love for her was a life's passion let loose, like a tulip breaking into height and colour after a long winter in frozen ground.

Their blissful interlude was broken, like a spell, when Daniel came home with what he thought was very good news: his first serious job offer.

'But it means moving to Beer Sheva,' said Monika, incredulously.

'Beer Sheva is not so bad. The heat is easier to take, not so humid. We can buy a nice apartment, bigger than this, have a baby . . .' Daniel was perfectly content with this fantasy. They would find a job for Monika, she would be just as happy there as she was in Tel Aviv.

So they moved, and Daniel's life immediately fell into place: he taught, wrote papers, even joined an eccentric group of local anarchists. But for Monika, there was nothing. No beach to distract her from her real life. No friends, not even fellow beach bums. Nothing to do except wait for Daniel. The town itself was barren, without the sparkle of the sea to soften its powdery dryness. Then came the war.

Monika indulged in a charmed life in Israel, oblivious of its tensions and dramas. She did not read the papers or watch the news. From her point of view, the war in the North was a mere background, more acoustic than visual. A distant thunderstorm. The military planes, on their way to the northern border and sometimes far beyond, violated the innocent Mediterranean sky, at increasingly frequent intervals. The bombs would explode elsewhere; mainly on the television screen.

When it was Daniel's turn to join his unit, she was shocked. How could something as absurd as a real war touch her own life!

'You're being very childish,' Daniel said, annoyed and impatient. 'It's not as if I wanted to leave you, or to hurt you. I'm against this war, don't you know? I *have* to go.'

She wanted to tell him that she needed time to get used to this abnormal lifestyle, that she couldn't picture her gentle Daniel, the historian, jumping from planes and invading enemy territory. Or even defending his own. But he was already in his paratrooper's uniform, red beret, red boots and all, machine gun and backpack in hand. Their last kiss was stained with that bit of anger they had been waiting for to give their marriage a seal of reality. She never saw him again.

This was three months ago. When they told her about Daniel's stupid death – the helicopter carrying him to his base crashed, for no apparent reason – she could not even cry. Overnight, she became the centre of everyone's solicitous attention: Daniel's family, her own parents, Daniel's friends and colleagues – everyone wanted to 'take her in' and help her mourn.

But Monika wanted to be left alone. Now that Daniel

was gone, she felt him everywhere. In the empty, dry bed, in the sandswept streets of this angular town, and, finally, in her abandoned soul. The desert, which she suddenly found strangely soothing, was the perfect place to bury her grief. Daniel had vanished from her life like a shadow, leaving her numb, unfocused. Leaving her famished, screaming for more.

3

The university offered her a job teaching German, but Monika said no. She could not go back to a paper life, hiding behind books and academic institutions and graded achievements. Instead, she chose to spend her days as a hairdresser's apprentice, sweeping locks of hair from underneath Jacques's feet. He knew nothing about her, didn't feel sorry for her, didn't even seem to see her.

Jacques, a loud, self-proclaimed genius, was hoping to make it to a great salon in Paris, in Rue St Honoré. Monika loved to watch him at work. Women – mothers, daughters – closed their eyes when he pressed them right into his groin if he felt like it, bending over their wet hair like a sculptor over heads of clay. They never tell him what they want, she noticed; they know he wouldn't listen. He wore white overalls over a beautiful dark brown body, white overalls and nothing else. He swore, sweated, drank arak. He'll miss this in Paris, if he ever gets there. And the war, she realized one day, the war just drones on, merging with the beats he plays in here, deafening, repetitive, electrifying.

Monika arrived very early one morning, hoping to avoid the heat. She found Jacques's stylish dungeon unlocked. Only Ahmed, the cleaner, was there, wiping the stone floor with a dripping mop. They nodded to each other, but did not exchange a word. Even in this small space, Ahmed had a way of appearing invisible, of retreating into the background. Occasionally, Monika felt a pair of eyes on her, a steady but blank gaze, expressing a mixture of admiration and something else. Hatred, maybe.

Shiny, muscular arms, broad back and chest, silence. But Monika knew, because Jacques had told her, that Ahmed was really a woman, a Bedouin. Disappearing into the city and changing her identity into that of a man was her way of escaping a brutal husband. 'She wants to forget she was ever a woman,' he had said, adding, with a wicked grin, 'don't you all.' Does a woman need more than the strength of Ahmed's arms to fight back, thought Monika.

She felt tired, even though the day had hardly begun. Her feet were heavy, as if she were carrying an enormous weight. Jacques's daily sycophantic audience would start arriving soon. He would attach his nicotine-stained fingers like magnets to their hair, touching them like a lover – a vicarious thrill to their senses, and a provocation to hers. Suddenly, she knew she couldn't face another second of clearing the floor of dark, curly tufts of hair, of washing laughing, chirping heads, of watching Jacques's self-satisfied reflection in the mirror. She sank into the nearest chair, and let her body go limp, her eyes hot.

'You shouldn't wear a lot of make-up,' Ahmed suddenly whispered in her ear. 'Do what we do – fill your eyes with black kohl, and let your tears do the rest. A black frame, that's all you need.'

Monika stared, hypnotized, as Ahmed's enormous sinewy arm made a cradle for her head. She broke down at the first brush of the Bedouin woman's rough skin against hers, and released all the grief she had been holding back for so long: for Daniel, and for Max, for herself, even for Ahmed, who rocked her gently, like a baby, until her eyes were dry again, and her strength returned.

By the time Jacques came in, she was gone. It was only eight in the morning, the sun already attacking the city, and the surrounding desert, like a mad arsonist. Even the sun is a fanatic in this crazy place, she thought. But she knew she could take it – as long as she moved back to the seashore.

It has to be said, for the record, that Max had predicted not only Monika's defection to Israel with Daniel, but also her widowhood. This did not require a supreme psychic talent, but only an average ability to tell a reasonably good story, combined with an informed knowledge of the Israeli political scene, and its likely toll on the lives of young men like Daniel Zohar.

What Max failed to foresee was Monika's pregnancy. It is hard to understand why, but the truth is that for some reason best understood by his analyst — if he had one — Max did not include that possibility in his mental calculations, and was caught off guard when Rabbi Krauthammer rang his door bell one Sunday and told him.

Krauthammer had not ostracized Max in the aftermath of the Reeperbahn affair. Instead, he had introduced him to 'the girls', and a peculiar friendship was born. 'Herr Kamenski', as the Israeli prostitutes insisted on calling him, became a frequent visitor and something of a spokesman for their plight when they ran into trouble with this or that authority. Krauthammer called him 'an intellectual pimp', and continued to tease him about his contrary, anaemic Jewishness. One of the girls, lovely, cross-eyed Tamar from Netanya, became the subject of Max's new novel, and he the occasional object of her expert attentions. So much so that she managed to persuade him that Rabbi Krauthammer was right: Max should get himself circumcised.

Krauthammer had refused to convert Monika, on the grounds that he did not 'do conversions', but he was perfectly willing to help Max with his painful rite. He arranged for a famous mohel to come from London, and, joining forces with a local surgeon of some renown, pronounced Max a proper son of Abraham. Max cursed his agnostic parents for not having done this to him when he was eight days old. But when he emerged from his swoon, bandaged and groggy, he found himself staring into the smiling faces of Tamar and her friends, and felt acutely, and inexplicably, happy. He had no idea why not having a foreskin should make him less prone to existential angst, but it did.

A downward glance revealed that his bandage had been tied like a ribbon, and coloured pink; he had been gift-wrapped. The girls, looking slightly guilty, burst out laughing, and so did Krauthammer. Max's next visit to the Reeperbahn would be highly experimental.

But this was some time ago. After a few months, the novelty wore off, and Max became a circumcised Jew like any other. He and Krauthammer now met every Sunday for tea, talked a little about Jews and Germany, and occasionally the rest of the world. But most of the time, they just sat together in Max's neat, book-lined room, and watched football.

Krauthammer did not want to deliver the news in any way that could be misinterpreted as meaningful. So he just said, in a neutral tone of voice, 'I heard from Monika's parents that she's coping well. The baby is due next month.'

Who can explain why Max responded to this brief statement with a deeper shock than even Krauthammer thought was possible? Or why he realized that he had to go and *see* Monika, not just phone her, as he did when he heard that Daniel was killed? Max could have asked Krauthammer but he knew that, not being a spiritual man, the rabbi would not attempt an explanation. He would simply say 'do' or 'don't do' – no reason given. Because that goddam rabbi just *knew* – right from wrong, truth from lie, important from irrelevant. And finding his way back to Monika was not wrong; it was important, and it was the only truth of his life.

She hardly looked pregnant when she met him at Ben Gurion airport. Monika's long, supple body carried the baby somewhere deep inside, somewhere out of sight, and she held him tight, without fear for her stomach. If it hadn't kicked, he wouldn't have believed it was there.

He wanted to talk to her about moving back to Hamburg, together, after the birth. Because he already knew that he could not live here, could not write here. But something about this Monika, who had been Daniel's wife, stopped him. She drove confidently through dark, hot streets, windows rolled down, the air full of heady smells and penetrating noises. When she stopped at a red light, he wanted to kiss her hand. But a little unfamiliar gesture – her fingers wiping droplets of sweat from her chin – took away his courage.

So instead of touching her, or saying what he had come here to say, he heard himself croak: 'By the way. Krauthammer won. I'm circumcised . . .'

Monika giggled. 'I know,' she said, without taking her eyes off the road. 'I met a woman called Tamar a few months ago – Krauthammer gave her my number – and I asked her to tie that ribbon – for me . . .'

Michael Farmer's Baby

God knows how I ended up giving birth to Michael Farmer's baby in a Catholic hospital in White Plains, New York, but I was glad I did. The two Irish midwives – Eileen and Erin – showered me with kindness, having absolutely nothing else to do. No other babies were struggling to be born that night, and we thought it was a good omen that all our names began with an 'e'. My name is Emma.

I used to be a nurse myself, a very long time ago, so I should have known better than to rush to the hospital just as soon as there was a tiny show of bloody mucus in my underwear. No water yet, and not a single contraction. But Eileen did not send me home. Maybe she realized that home was a terrifying place to be; I had arrived alone, unlike most mothers these days, looking tired and middle-aged. Women tend to bring a small bag with them when they enter maternity wards; I was pushing a large, heavy suitcase, containing most of my belongings. If it hadn't been such an elegant piece of luggage, I'm sure they would have suspected me of being homeless. Later I would tell Eileen and Erin how I had followed Professor Michael Farmer and his family around the world, until we ended up back in his home town. Then they picked up and moved again, to England, but I was stuck, with my pregnant belly and twenty years' worth of memories of loving a serious, disciplined man who never stopped being devoted to his wife, yet thrilled to his secretary's touch. My touch.

Eileen was the older, motherly one, thick reddish-brown hair plaited and tied like a tiara on top of her head, warm freckled face, warm hands. She radiated confidence and solid calm. Erin was a sexy dynamo, with a shiny blonde bob, pale skin, strong blue eyes, amazing curves under her bland white uniform.

The stern-faced doctor gave Eileen a quizzical look when she said, with a ringing lilt, 'We might as well keep her overnight,' but didn't seem surprised at her willingness to look after a woman who was not even in labour. He muttered that I was free to eat and drink whatever I liked, and disappeared. We didn't see him again until the very end.

'So, where's the father?' Erin asked me, cheerfully. Eileen frowned at her and handed me a glass of water.

But I was immune to insensitive questions. In fact, I was dying to tell them.

'Gone to England,' I said. 'He doesn't even know I'm having his child. He's married and . . .' I shut up, suddenly remembering where I was. Would they throw me out?

Eileen only nodded, gravely, and Erin beamed a glorious smile in my direction: 'So, where're you from? White Plains?'

'Boston. By the way, my grandparents came from Ireland.'

'Well, we figured you were an Irish American, your last name being O'Connor. Where in Ireland?'

'From a small seaside town called Newcastle. That's County Down, isn't it? Near the Mourne Mountains. My grandfather always talked about them. And there is this old song—'

'I know it, I know it!' squealed Erin. She looked at Eileen, registering her benevolent smile, took a deep breath and sang:

> Oh, Mary, this London's a wonderful sight
> With people here working by day and by night
> They don't sow potatoes nor barley nor wheat
> But there's gangs of them diggin' for gold in the street
> At least when I asked them, that's what I was told
> So I just took a hand at this diggin' for gold

But for all that I've found there, I might as well be
In the place where the dark Mourne sweeps down to
the sea.

Her clear voice was full of fun, like the words she was singing, but her eyes carried the gentle sadness of the tune. Erin stopped herself, with difficulty. 'I know the whole song,' she said, glowing with self-satisfaction. 'My boyfriend has a website of Irish folk music.'

I felt a back pain, a mild one, but decided to ignore it.

'Stop showing off,' said Eileen. 'I'm sure Emma is not interested in your singing. Are you comfortable, dear?'

'But I'm *very* interested,' I said. 'The man I worked for was a sociologist, and this was his area. The Victorian period, I mean.'

Erin's attention drifted, I saw, so I changed the subject: 'And where are you from?'

'We're both from Cork.'

This hospital, it turned out, had a long-standing tradition of bringing in nurses from Ireland, with a direct link to their nursing college in Dublin. 'But I was going to leave anyway,' said Eileen. 'Me too,' said Erin.

For some reason, this made us erupt in silly giggles, like a bunch of teenage girls. I felt another pull in my lower back, as if an unskilled novice was trying to give me a massage. I wanted to forget that I was here to give birth to a child. I would just talk, and talk, and eventually I would go home and live as I had lived before. Or maybe I could stay here for ever with Eileen and Erin, they made me feel so good . . .

'Come, walk with me,' said Eileen. She had noticed my clenched fist.

Erin went to make tea and sandwiches, while I leaned on Eileen, like an old woman, and moved about the dimly lit, empty maternity ward.

'Talk to me,' I said, my breath returning to normal. 'Did you bring your family with you?'

'Oh no,' said Eileen. 'I'm not married, and all my brothers and sisters are back in—'

'Cork?' I interrupted.

'No, England. London, and Liverpool.' She sighed. 'The hard thing is to leave Ireland. Once you've left, it doesn't matter where you go.'

Then I told her about my early nursing days, in Boston. And how I met Michael Farmer, then a much younger man, when he brought his small son to the emergency room with a twisted ankle. How we started talking about this and that, mainly about his interesting research, and before I knew it, I had resigned from my job at the hospital and accepted his invitation to work for him as his private secretary and assistant. I didn't mind: my father was in the process of drinking himself to death, and I was expected to look after him. I needed to get away, and make myself unavailable to my family. So, almost overnight, I had a new life: typing Michael Farmer's books and papers and filing his collection of facts and ideas about Victorian England. I tried to explain to Eileen, in carefully chosen words, that although we never really spent a night together, Professor Farmer and I were addicted to each other. Ten minutes stolen away from dictating his latest discovery about, say, Victorian contraception would be enough to make him shed his reptilian skin and turn me inside out. He was a harsh, dry man, but I was crazy about him. I had never had a lover before, or since. I've always been invisible to men, and to women for that matter, but Michael Farmer gave me a chance, and wasn't disappointed. If I have a mission in life, it is to tell the world that plain-looking women are worth a second, and third, glance.

'Do you mean the sponge?' asked Eileen. My contractions seemed to have stopped, and we sat down to drink the tea Erin had brought. 'I heard they used some kind of sponge.'

I told them that Victorian women were advised to first attach 'a bobbin' to a piece of large sponge, before inserting it in the vagina, and to 'make it damp to hold the sperm'. I even read somewhere that 'an English Duchess never goes out to dinner without it'!

Eileen put down her cup, looked straight into my eyes and smiled: 'How do you know this? I don't believe it!'

'Oh, I've read so much about it, even some private diaries . . . It's really amazing how *open* the Victorians were, compared to what we think of them.'

'Open?' asked Eileen, incredulously. 'I thought they were terrible prudes.'

'Like you,' teased Erin.

'Oh, I'm no prude,' Eileen protested, in earnest self-defence. 'If I sound a bit strict sometimes, it's because I've seen, with my own eyes, what happens when all the fun is over. And because I don't believe it's that much fun to begin with. As my grandmother used to say: "Three things that leave the shortest traces: a bird on a branch, a ship on the sea, and a man on a woman."'

'Oh, but it is fun!' Erin resisted. '*I* think it is.' She slid down to the very edge of the chair, stretched her long legs before her, crossed them slowly at the ankles and patted her knees, lovingly. Even in the bulky shoes she was wearing, Erin made you think of cinematic bedroom scenes, or silent hospital sex à la *ER*; I could just imagine her being cast against, say, George Clooney, who would be allowed to grope for her dark pubic ringlets under a morbid display of chest X-rays . . .

'Well, Emma here is a good example of . . .' Eileen started to argue, passionately, but suddenly checked herself. She was clearly afraid of involving me in their discussion, in case it affected my mood.

'Anyway, back to the Victorians,' I said, to ease the slight tension between them. I asked Erin to wheel my suitcase over to where we were sitting. My laptop was under a messy pile of clothes I had managed to throw in before leaving for hospital. The research I'd compiled for my boss was filed under Farmer/Victoriana. I quickly found the quote I was looking for: 'Love is a subject on which some women will not talk . . . It is a barbarous custom that forbids the maid to make an advance in love, or that confines that advance to the eye, the fingers . . . Why should not the female state her passion to the male, as well as the male to the female?' This was written in a book entitled *Every Woman's Book; or, What is Love?*, published in London in 1826. Erin was impressed. 'You see!' she said to Eileen. 'Even the Victorians were more advanced than you!'

Now, Eileen was really hurt. 'When did I ever say you couldn't show a man how you felt about him? Honestly,' she said, turning to me, 'this girl will make you think I'm a monster. As if I haven't had my share of . . .' Again, she broke off, in mid-sentence. I was beginning to feel that the unspoken halves of her sentences would add up to quite a story.

I was also beginning to feel just a little guilty. There

was no sign of any contractions whatsoever, I was a bit tired but otherwise very comfortable. Maybe I should just let them have their sleep, and go home?

'Oh no, don't you worry about that,' said Eileen, with calm authority in her strong voice. 'You'll be giving birth soon all right, and we are on night duty anyway. Let me examine you, just in case.'

She took me into the examination room and checked, gently, whether I had opened up.

'That's funny,' she said, 'you aren't dilated at all, but you say you have had a few contractions?'

'Well, just a couple, maybe,' I said. Just then, I had a third one. This spasm was stronger, but ebbed off faster than the others.

'Would you like to sleep for a bit? You'll need your strength for later,' Erin said, barely suppressing a yawn.

But I was afraid of dozing off. For me, there was terrible loneliness in sleep, always had been, and today – tonight – I could not face it. I stood up again, as quickly as I could, and pretended to feel no tiredness whatsoever.

'Walking is good for you,' said Eileen, as we resumed our slow rounds of the ward, with Erin accompanying us this time.

'So, tell us some more about all this gory Victorian stuff. I love it!' she said, a bit too loudly. 'I can just see those prim ladies with their fancy dresses. Imagine: a

Duchess in her carriage, on her way to a dinner party, suddenly ordering the driver to turn back: she forgot her *sponge*!'

Even Eileen was amused by this picture. Encouraged, Erin ran a little ahead of us, faced us and started singing the second stanza of 'The Mountains of Mourne':

> I believe that when writin' a wish you expressed
> As to how the fine ladies in London were dressed
> Well if you believe me, when asked to a ball
> They don't wear no tops to their dresses at all
>
> Don't be startin' them fashions now, Mary McRee,
> Where the Mountains of Mourne sweep down to
>   the sea.

'I don't think Mary McRee would have known about the sponge,' I said.

'Who is Mary McRee?' asked Eileen.

'Just a name,' Erin laughed. 'Just a name for any Irish girl back home. Am I right?'

I said she was, sort of. But then I added: 'Except that thousands of "Marys" ended up joining their families in England or America. Very often, they left on their own, mostly as servant girls.'

'Yeah, I know. That's what would have happened to us, if we had been alive in those days,' said Erin. Suddenly, she sounded almost mournful.

I was tired of walking. I suggested that we sit down again – they both seemed pleased about that – and, feeling somehow responsible for entertaining them, I decided to talk about the most fascinating case I had ever researched for Michael Farmer. I told them about Mary O'Shea, the very young bride who murdered her husband two weeks after their wedding. Now I had both my midwives' complete attention.

The magic, I knew, was in the words 'young bride' and 'murder'. I had felt it myself, when I first came across them in an old Victorian scrapbook in the British Library.

Actually, Michael Farmer was never really curious about the details of this case. He had only asked me to dig up any real-life, non-literary documents about women in Victorian England; he was particularly interested in official papers and letters. I remember waiting patiently at one of the oak desks, watching the rows of hunched shoulders and heads bent in serious concentration. The peacefulness of the Reading Room made me reflect on the relatively pleasant life I led, considering that I had enslaved myself, possibly forever, to a man who had better things to do than think about me, even in his spare time. I loved him, of course, but I also hated him desperately for being a free person – something I could never be. I fantasized about what would happen if his wife died, suddenly, of natural causes, or of a small but deadly accident; would he turn to me, finally, for life-long succour, or would I continue to live in the very margins of his orderly existence, following him wherever he chose to go? Sometimes, I could think and very nearly talk like a character in a cheap Victorian romance. I could get really excited by the idea of having *no choice* in life but to *obey* my *destiny*, as defined by a man's passionate interest in my heaving cleavage, my wan cheeks and my burning, probably not very fragrant body buried and constrained under so many layers of velvety, satiny, silky fabrics.

The librarian arrived with a small pile of books and papers, and the information that one of the manuscripts I had ordered was actually a brittle scrapbook, which could only be viewed in a separate room upstairs. This was a compilation, by an unknown person, of facts pertaining to the case of a Mary O'Shea: newspaper cuttings, poems, songs. The first clipping was an invitation to the public to come and witness Mary O'Shea's execution. The girl, who was 'in her eighteenth year', was to be 'publicly strangled' at a London jail by 'the HANGMAN, the Great Moral Teacher, who, after fastening her arms to her side, and putting a rope round her neck, will strike the scaffold from under her, and if the neck of the wretched victim be not by shock broken, the said MORAL TEACHER will pull the legs of the miserable girl until by his weight and strength united he STRANGLES HER.' Admission to this

'GRAND MORAL SPECTACLE for the instruction of a Christian people' was free. The year was 1851.

It must have been the veiled sexual sadism of the announcement, disguised as a lesson in religious righteousnesss, that aroused my immediate sympathy with the young murderess: the public as a virtuous voyeur, deriving instant moral gratification and, I was sure, instant orgasms from watching Mary O'Shea's passive submission to her executioner.

I read on in order to find out what crime she had committed to deserve such gruesome punishment, and discovered that Mary had been accused of murdering her husband, Peter O'Shea, two weeks after their wedding, by poisoning a dumpling with arsenic.

Again, I found myself identifying with her, for no obvious reason. And I was not alone; after she was convicted, petitions were circulated and many signatures collected, appealing that her life be spared, because of her sex and age. Women signed a special, separate petition to Queen Victoria, hoping for the royal clemency. It was rejected.

To everyone's amazement, Mary was extraordinarily composed at the hanging. She received her sacrament with calm, and walked to the drop unsupported, with a firm step. The crowd was 'struck with awe', especially when, in her last moments, she scanned the assembled mass of people – men, women, children – with an astounding air of determination. Or was it defiance? I had no way of knowing. But the more I read about the case, the more it seemed to me like a delicious, unresolved mystery. Not like a detective novel – more like an enigmatic set of circumstances which, if explained, might shed some light on . . . I wasn't sure on what exactly, but I felt that Mary's short life had a peculiar relevance to my own.

Her death was terrible. She struggled, painfully, for a long time before it was over. The crowd was horrified, and cried 'shame, shame!' and 'murder, murder!'

'I wonder if the mothers covered their children's eyes, the way we do today when they are watching violence or sex on television,' said Eileen.

The three of us sat silent for quite a while. I couldn't guess what they were thinking; Erin looked dreamy, slightly troubled and distant. Eileen seemed to be digesting, slowly, what I had told them. Finally, she asked me what I had often wondered myself: why all this sympathy? Mary O'Shea was, after all, a ruthless killer.

'Who was she, anyway?' Erin wanted to know.

'Good question. The scrapbook was a patchy source of information about Mary O'Shea, as were the newspapers from that period. She wasn't famous, she wasn't rich, she wasn't even middle-class. She was a poor Irish peasant girl, who had come to London from a small village in Ulster, like so many others. She may have wanted to get away from the famine, poverty, hopelessness. Or she may have simply followed the newly opened route of migration, of change. I don't know. Her oldest brother had left first and gone to work as a labourer in Liverpool. When he moved to London, where he could get better wages, the rest of the family followed. Mary was one of seven children. Her youngest brother, eight-year-old Patrick, was the main witness at the trial.'

I described how they all shared a room, together with another family, in a narrow alley in Whitechapel. By my calculations, there would have been fifteen people in that room, including children of all ages, including a dying grandmother and two very sick infants. The women tried hard to keep everything clean, but it would have been an impossible task. There was little light, the alley stank of sewage, barefooted, grimy children filled the street, with some mothers looking on from dilapidated doorways and windows. On dry days, shabby shoes lined the pavement.

Luckily for Mary and the others, she didn't have to suffer this new kind of poverty for very long. She found a position as a servant girl with an English family in Bury St Edmunds. She was sixteen years old at the time.

'OK, I know what happened next,' interrupted Eileen. 'She was seduced by her master.'

I didn't answer.

'Well?' she persisted.

'I'm not sure, actually. Nobody knows what really happened while she was in service. But, statistically speaking, there is every chance that that would have been a very likely scenario.'

Actually, I had come to the same conclusion myself. By all accounts, Mary was a 'good-looking country girl', with light hair, large blue eyes, a thin face and figure. I imagined this scene: her master, a clerk named Jeremiah Ward, walks into his bedroom and finds her bent over his bed, tying the bows on a fresh pillowcase. She feels his arms around her waist, his breath on her neck. She is petrified, and excited. But is she really surprised? No. Because she has been expecting it, from the very first day.

'So, do you think she encouraged him?' whispered Erin.

I could just see Erin as Mary, and I knew that *she* would have wished for that encounter to happen, would have fantasized about it until it became a reality. Just as I had done with Michael Farmer . . .

'How can I answer that?' I said. 'But I do have a feeling, from what I've read, that she did like him. Maybe she even loved him. Otherwise, why would she have wanted to visit him after the wedding?'

'She did *what?*' Erin seemed very stimulated by this unexpected piece of information.

'Mary was in service with the Wards for two years,' I explained. 'Towards the end of her second year, while she was visiting her family for Christmas, Peter O'Shea, whom she had known from childhood – they were from the same village in Ireland, and he was a close friend of her older brother's – asked her to marry him. Mary's parents pressed her to accept quickly; Peter was a good, reliable young man, also a railroad labourer, like her brother. It meant moving back into her family lodgings after the wedding, with her new husband.

'Mary agreed, but asked to be allowed to visit the Wards before the wedding. Peter said he would be happier if she didn't, but suggested that she could go after the wedding, instead. What was he afraid of? Did he know? *Was* there anything to know? All I can say is that the wedding took place, and everything seemed fine. One day, about a week after they were married, Mary travelled to Bury St Edmunds, as she had requested. She did not stay with the Wards this time, but with an aunt who lived nearby. Some claimed that when she returned home from that visit, she was a changed person. Withdrawn, subdued. Not that she had ever been a very lively girl – there was always an air of heavy earnestness about her. (So maybe she was more like a young Eileen than like Erin, I thought.) But now she seemed burdened, even sad. A week later, she served Peter his usual evening meal – dumplings, bread, tea. He became violently sick, and complained of terrible heartburn. Mary and her mother tried to make him feel better, by giving him some brandy, I think, but nothing helped. He died in the early hours of the morning. The post-mortem found a ruptured artery, and it was also said that he died of English cholera. Nobody suspected that he had been poisoned, until two dogs died after eating something off the dunghill where the mother had emptied the bowl into which Peter had vomited. The body was then exhumed and arsenic poisoning was found to be the cause of Peter O'Shea's death. Mary's little brother had seen her cook and serve the food, and she did not deny her guilt at all. She gave a written confession, which was not to be made public until after she was gone.'

'What did she say in the confession?' Erin asked, breathlessly.

'Just the technical details of her crime,' I said. 'She explained how she bought the poison at the shop of Mr H. Wilkinson, chemist, in Bury St Edmunds, during her last visit there. He knew her well, because Mrs Ward often sent Mary to his shop on errands. Nobody had persuaded her to do it; she had acted alone. She had no complaints against her husband; she simply never loved him, and wished to go back to service. "I do not wish to live," she wrote, "for I never could be happy in this world; . . . I hope through a sincere repentance of my sins . . . to be received into Heaven."

'While she was in jail, she remained silent on the motive of her crime. She was visited, regularly, by her priest, but did not open up to him, nor to her mother. When they took down her body after the hanging, they found a note to her mother in the folds of her dress, which she had scribbled secretly in prison. It only said, in more affectionate terms, what she had stated in her confession: that she was happy to die. That she had hated her life in London. That she was treated well by her family, and her husband, but what did that mean when all of them together lived as lower than the lowest creatures. "I never see the moon, or the sun in London," she had written. "Our Irish moon was like a Christmas sweet in the sky." She had nothing to look forward to, except more drudgery, more hunger, illness, death and filth. And so, she told her mother in her childish handwriting and in simple words, she hoped that she would go to Heaven, and be free of this life.

'And that,' I said, 'is what intrigued me more than anything else about the case. I mean the fact that when Mary O'Shea had to think about what she had done, her only tool would have been religion. And the same goes for public opinion, the jury, the judge, the press, her family, her executioner – and her priest, of course. Today, there are so many other layers between what happens to us, and how we interpret it. We have psychology, psycho-analysis, psychiatry, genetics. So there is the possibility that a young, displaced girl like Mary, living in terrible conditions, may have been abused, suicidally depressed, schizophrenic – anything but simply "guilty."'

'Wow, you're really involved in this business,' said Erin. 'You've really thought about it a lot.'

She may have been telling me that she'd had enough of this particular story, but I wasn't done yet. I had never shared my thoughts on Mary's case with anyone, and needed to hear what Eileen and Erin would make of it.

'Tell me what you think of this,' I said quietly, with some hesitation. 'While she was working for the Wards, Mary discovered the joys of sex, by sleeping with Mr Ward. Maybe he didn't treat her well as a servant – after all, she was just an Irish girl doing some dirty work – but he wasn't so bad as a lover, having had a lot of experience. Because before he married Mrs Ward, whoever *she* was, he'd had many other flings, maybe with other servants. In any case, he was sort of good at it. So they had a routine: on the days when she changed the sheets on his bed, he dirtied them one more time, with her. No trace was left of their love act. It was swallowed in the large bundle of laundry Mary carried down the stairs afterwards. And then she gets married to a kind man who loves her, maybe, but is an uncouth, rough lover. After the first few nights with him, she can't stand the thought of it. She goes back to Bury, to tell Jeremiah Ward how unhappy she is. He manages to seduce her, one more time, and suggests, jokingly, that she could do away with her husband and come back to work for him. But Mary is hooked on the idea; she finds a church to pray in – not her own Catholic church, but the Church of England, St Mary's, because it's closer to the chemist's shop in the main square where she is about to get the arsenic. She looks up at the serene wooden angels supporting the dark wood ceiling, and thinks: no matter what happens, I will soon be where they are. Death is a soothing thought to her at that moment, whichever way she looks at it. Death has no finality for her. It is a transition. It's like . . . like coming home.'

Erin had actually nodded off during my speech, but Eileen jumped in as soon as I gave her a chance: 'You've got a very vivid imagination, my dear. But has it ever occurred to you that your Mary might have been raped by that repulsive Mr Ward, or that she was pregnant, and didn't want her husband to find out? I've seen plenty of such cases myself, you know. Or,' she added quickly before I could respond, 'that she was simply an evil girl?'

'But what does "evil" mean?' I said. 'How does it differ from being very, very messed up?'

Erin opened her eyes, suddenly: 'Did you ever figure out who the scrapbook belonged to? A man, or a woman? I would love to know!'

That's when I fainted, apparently. Not for long, but it was enough to give my midwives a bit of a scare, and to put me to bed. I loved the sound of those words: 'my midwives'. It was sweet, it meant safety, a haven. And I was incredibly lucky to have them all to myself. I would have been jealous if I had had to share them with other mothers-to-be.

I was left alone for a few moments. Lying on my side, as I had been instructed by Eileen, I noticed a wooden crucifix above the door. Not a very large one, but big enough to remind me that pretty soon, I would have a lot of praying to do. And afterwards, a huge confession. The funny thing was that I did not feel like talking to a priest. I felt like talking to Eileen. About Michael Farmer, and the baby.

'Emma,' said Eileen, softly, 'this is Doctor Fitzgerald. You met him before. Don't worry, he just wants to ask you a few questions.'

Dr Fitzgerald's voice was not quite as soft as Eileen's when he asked me how I had managed to fool the hospital, and why.

I tried to look surprised, but when Erin hugged me and whispered, go on, tell us, it's OK, I broke down. The first question was easy to answer: I avoided medical examinations by not having a steady address. The first doctor I had gone to, after the Farmers left for England and I had lost my job with him, simply took my word for it when I said that I had missed my period and that my pregnancy test was positive. With that information in my files, I kept moving around, enjoying my symptoms: I ate for two, and my stomach grew with amazing speed. I had morning sickness, I craved pickles and ice cream, I bought lovely maternity clothes and baby gear. I read all the relevant books, and identified with everything they said. I cried with joy when I felt the baby move, just the way it was supposed to – like a little butterfly fluttering about my insides, waiting to come out. I did know, deep down, that it was a phantom pregnancy, but it didn't feel unreal to me. I truly believed that one day, I would give birth to Michael Farmer's baby.

But the second question – *why* had I done it? – I could not answer at all.

Inhaling New York

Sasha realized that although her son was almost fifteen years old, he had never heard of Karl Marx. Nor had he read *Portnoy's Complaint*. She knew she was up against a powerful opponent – the brainless, throbbing pop culture of the '90s – but she decided that whatever other kind of heritage she wasn't allowed to pass on to her eldest, she would at least break through his resistance and open his eyes to the existence of a couple of great books.

Karl Marx was almost a failure, but not quite. Jon refused to read him outright – 'too many pages without dialogue, Mum' – but was extremely impressed with the slogan 'Religion is the opium of the masses'. 'He said *that*? That's really decent. Wicked.' And he took the sentence, if not the thought, to his bedroom, where he and his friends tried to transform it into a rap song, rhyming 'masses' with 'asses' to a rhythmic accompaniment of explosive farting noises. Their laughter, loud and rowdy and already very male, shook the house, shook the world, and made her feel ancient, like a volcano that never erupted.

But she *had* erupted, and not once but twice. The first time, at twenty, when she decided never to have any children but to have many men instead. Manhattan was barely big enough to contain her happy promiscuity. For year after cheerful year, she turned friends into lovers and back into friends – to make room for new lovers. There were those she talked to incessantly – about Marx, about *Portnoy's Complaint* among other things – and there were others who excited her because they came from worlds she didn't know and whose language she didn't speak – her parents' Mexican gardener, taxi drivers of all nationalities, even an occasional all-American pizza delivery boy. She was thinking about literature and philosophy, and sleeping with men without thinking. Each new adventure made her feel more in control, and she became addicted to one-night stands like a compulsive housewife to constant spring-cleaning.

Her sedate parents, safely ensconced in Westchester, applauded her academic progress and, comparing the new Sasha with the grim, placid high school girl they remembered and never understood, praised her 'impressive personal development' (her father's heavy words). But Sasha's bubbly vitality had more to do with her seismic love life than with the degrees she accumulated. She was intoxicated by her giddy freedom, she loved her cocky confidence, she even loved her own lanky beauty. In those heady days, she would look at her naked reflection in a mirror, a man's sweat and semen still on her skin, and smile at herself with drunken delight: life was a cinch. She wished she hadn't wasted her suburban adolescence in such agonizing seriousness.

And then she met Jack, her very attractive, very quiet neighbour. She tried to exploit their occasional silent encounters in the elevator or in the laundry room by drawing him into flirtatious conversations – and failed. He seemed not to see her. In his presence, she felt like a ghost trying to make herself visible to the living. She began losing interest in all other men and found herself focusing entirely on the one man she clearly could *not* have. Her playfulness left her, bit by painful bit. Her seriousness returned. Sasha was madly in love, with a strange man who was oblivious of her existence.

Or so she thought. In actual fact, Jack was not all that peculiar. He was English. A journalist with a difficult mission – to cover New York for a British Sunday magazine, without giving away the embarrassing fact that he loved the city he was reporting from, and strongly disliked his own home territory. His paper expected an anti-American stance from him about American poverty and violence, the crudity of American culture, the American desire to take over the world. Jack's pieces were meant to show how much of the New York apple was rotten at the core. He did his job admirably – but in secret, wrote other pieces, hiding them in a locked desk drawer, like an East European samizdat writer. Those secret essays were, he knew, quite wonderful, much better than anything he had ever published. They were about small things, but added up to a passionate homage to New York, and to America. He wrote about the exhilaration he felt in Grand Central, when an all-black string quartet played Bach and Mozart, and the entire station froze and applauded. The applause came from everywhere, even from 'the balcony' – the waiting area under the ceiling. He wrote about the kids break-dancing in the streets long before break dance became a regular staple of world pop culture. He wrote about two elderly women on the subway, holding bouquets of wilting flowers they had just cut in their daughters' suburban gardens, talking about their occasional visits to the daughters' homes which didn't feel like homes to them, the mothers.

He also wrote about how, at the end of each day, he could not fall asleep because the city was always wide awake and didn't seem to follow the laws of nature. Jack was from a small village in Devon and liked to feel in tune with the natural rhythm of daybreaks and sunsets.

He liked to give in to seasonal moodswings, to the highs and lows of a winter or summer solstice. The permanent buzz and noise of New York's hyperactive streets gave him terrible insomnia, which drained all his energy and turned him into a bit of a zombie.

Sasha's perception of Jack's indifference to her presence was not exactly right. It was not that he did not see her, or appreciate her good looks. He did. But he was too tired, not too blasé, to do anything about it. He spent his days and nights walking around New York, *inhaling* New York, and by the time he returned to his building in East Village, he was in a pleasant, dazed state of well-deserved exhaustion.

Back in his stuffy one-room apartment, he would quickly tear off his clothes and jump in the shower. In the summer, he didn't bother drying himself and fell wet into the always unmade bed, praying for instant sleep. But after a fitful hour which felt more like a minute, he would be wide awake again, for the rest of the night. Then he would sit at his desk, drenched in sweat, and write another never-to-be published tribute to the city which was killing him, softly.

Sasha decided to take action. She *would* meet this man, at least once. She had a radical plan, which was in fact a carbon copy of her own Russian grandmother's courting of the aloof man who was to become Sasha's grandfather. It worked a couple of generations ago, in another culture, so why not here and now?

The plan involved asking the super to inform Mr Jack Fitzherbert of Apt 7A that Miss Alexandra (Sasha) Goldstein in Apt 11C had found a few articles of Mr Fitzherbert's laundry in the basement, and would he be kind enough to come and collect them *this evening between ten and eleven*. Jack hadn't been aware of having lost any of his laundry, but thanked the super and knocked on Sasha's door that night. 'It's open!' she said, trying to sound very matter-of-fact. He hesitated, then pushed the door open and found a very pretty, very naked woman spread out on the living-room couch, which doubled as her bed. She looked familiar and inviting enough for him to respond the way Sasha's grandfather had responded to her grandmother. Both women had eventually, after much glorious lovemaking, sat up with a huge smile on their young faces, thinking: 'Well, that was that.'

And so it was. Jack could not spend another day without Sasha, who had inadvertently solved his insomnia problem. But he also discovered that they had much in common and a great deal to talk about. He was no longer alone on his walks around New York. Sasha took him to clubs and secluded corners even he had never seen, and introduced him to her bohemian Marxist friends. She took him to see her suburban parents, describing him as 'the man from downstairs'. Which was just as well, because a few months later, Jack's assignment was over and he had to go back to London. He begged Sasha to marry him, to move to London with him. He needed her in order to maintain his connection with New York, the way James Joyce had his portable Ireland in his wife Nora wherever he lived. And so they moved to London, and whenever they made love, Jack imagined himself fucking all those New York women whose faces and bodies he was desperately trying not to forget.

Sasha's love for him diminished, very slowly at first, then with lightning speed, as he gradually retreated into a polite, formal shell of a man. He became a hack writer at his paper, writing mainly about cars and lifestyles. His New York essays lay forgotten in a particularly messy drawer of his desk.

Sasha's first year in London was a bit like Jack's infatuation with New York. She wandered around the city, bus-hopping, as she called it, ending up in unfamiliar areas and thinking that London could generate almost as much buzz as New York, but for some reason didn't manage it. She started working as a research assistant for a political scientist at the LSE, but had to stop because her first pregnancy was a nightmare. She was forced to spend most of it in bed, so she read and reread everything she could get her hands on – including Jack's secret writing. The only issue she refused to think or read about was the fact that she was about to become a mother.

When the baby, a boy, was finally born, in a manner far less traumatic than she had anticipated, Sasha made the startling discovery that she was unwilling to name it. That is, she was unwilling to choose one name from what seemed like a vortex of identities. To name the child would be to give it character, to put it in a context, to acknowledge its existence as a person and her own new role in life. Well, it's still *my* life, she thought, as she stared at her son's tiny clenched fists. She had six weeks to decide, according to the law of the land, and she would take her time.

Jack was going crazy, but tried to hide his impatience behind a veneer of stony-faced self-control. He proposed two names: a Jewish one, to honour Sasha's roots, and an English one, to honour his own. Samuel (to be nicknamed Sam), and Julius – no nickname.

'Bullshit,' said Sasha. 'Over my dead body.'

'OK, darling, so what do you suggest?'

She hated him when he called her darling. It was his way of humouring her nascent insanity.

'Don't know yet. There is time.'

But weeks went by and the agonizing search for a name continued. They stopped speaking to each other in the evenings, except to call out names they had thought of that day.

'Cyrus.'

'Tadeusz.'

'Nicholas.'

'Daniel.'

'Peter.'

'Shmuel.'

After a while, Sasha recognised the pattern behind her indecision. It was the same force that had propelled her towards promiscuity, and made her want to fuck every attractive man she could lay her hands on. Choosing only one of them meant having to settle, to compromise, to perpetrate the unforgivable sin of family boredom. And here she was, finally trapped in the same cycle. The least she could do was rebel by not naming this poor child. He can choose his own name when he grows up.

When she said that, Jack stopped fuming in silent anger and slapped her across the face. Then he stared at his own hand in disbelief and started crying, joining the baby who was already screaming his head off with hunger.

Suddenly, there was bliss in the air. Sasha returned the slap, gently, and bounced back into a fairly normal version of herself. She picked up the purple-faced infant and, as he began sucking at her enormous dark nipple, rocked back and forth in the armchair, thinking. Then she said:

'I know. Let's call him Ninel.'

'Ninel?? What kind of a name is that?'

'You know. Lenin in reverse. To honour my heritage.'

They argued, very quietly, so as not to upset the baby. The six weeks were up the next morning. So was the prohibition against postnatal intercourse.

As it turned out, 'Ninel' was not a legally acceptable option. The name simply did not exist, according to the friendly clerk they went to see in order to register their son's name. Not on any of the local lists of names, including the many 'ethnic' ones. They could keep it as a second name, but not as the child's first given name. So, what was it to be?

Jack looked at his wife in despair. He had that 'frankly my dear I don't give a damn' look, which threatened to develop into something a little more dramatic.

'Jonathan,' said Sasha, without consulting him. 'Just Jonathan.'

This naming was the beginning of her initiation into life as it has been lived for hundreds of generations. She gradually learned to fade into the background as her children began to take over. When she tried to tell them how little they knew, they laughed. When she tried to convince them that their parents had both been *truly alive* long before they had even thought of becoming parents or lovers, they laughed and giggled and left the room. They had a point.

But suddenly, as she listened to her son's musical take on Marx, she'd had enough. She stormed out and quickly ran to the nearest bookshop. Luckily, they had three copies of *Portnoy's Complaint* in stock. She bought them all, raced down the two leafy blocks back to her house and up the two flights of stairs into Jon's room. His friends were still there, experimenting with a new thumping sound. She pretended to ignore it, even though she loved the way it pulsated through her mind and body, and handed each of them a copy of the book.

Once he had read Roth, she would give Jon his father's New York essays, which she had typed up and cried over when Jack died, after the birth of their second child. And then they would both be ready to talk.

Bad Writing

Last time I got mugged on the subway, the guy said: Pull it off, pull it off. But I couldn't, even though my hands were so sweaty I left stains all over my grey silk skirt when I tried to hide the ring between my knees and under my thighs. He spotted it right away, as soon as I reached for my loops. I didn't care if he took those. I didn't care about anything, I just wanted it to be over, and I wanted him to get off that train, loaded with other people's things, and goodbye.

But the ring wouldn't come off, because I'm not the person I was when I got married. And I'm not just talking about my weight. At twenty-two, I was sun-tanned, invincibly stupid and determined to marry my dying best friend's middle-aged husband. Now, at forty-two, I am excessively Rubensesque, pale, in spite of this being the height of another New York summer, and, by general consensus, a person worth talking to. The husband is indeed mine and pushing sixty, and if I didn't have my dog I'd be the loneliest person in the world.

It's a distinctive ring, in a dramatic white-and-yellow gold mixture sort of way. James had insisted that I wear it. Two brides, one ring. The funny thing was that Diana knew about it, and didn't mind. In fact, she slipped it off her pencil-thin, translucent finger herself, when she started losing it in her bedsheets every time she moved (which wasn't very often). Diana was twenty-two when she died. I would never have married James if she hadn't.

It started with the little postcard Diana sent me from New York. We hadn't seen each other since that last cigarette we'd shared in the students' smoking room in our high school in Hamburg, just before writing the final exam. These were the free '70s and we were given special smoking privileges in the school. Diana smoked Gitanes, strong stuff, and looked a bit like an unfinished version of Lauren Bacall. She had style and lots of plans, all of which had to do with going to live in New York and being totally, absolutely free. She hated her very friendly, very formal parents, who, apparently, also hated each other. She said she wanted to be surrounded by millions of aggressive, hot-blooded strangers. Hence New York.

The postcard only said:

Dear Paula

James (my husband) will pay for your ticket and everything else if you come here and stay with us for the summer. Call me collect. *Please* call.

Diana

I didn't even know she was married. We were both only twenty-one at the time. I did phone. James's voice was friendly and formal – not unlike her parents' except in English. Diana was very ill and needed a friend 'from home'. No, not her parents. She asked only for me, said I was the only person she could stand having around. Would I come?

I had been considering some sort of non-descript job with a local tabloid paper, nothing exciting. The sort of thing that is supposed to 'open doors'. A summer away didn't seem to matter, my mother and stepfather didn't care, so I agreed.

James Painter (the 3rd, as it turned out) was a wealthy, angular man, very tall and polite, and ice-cold. The story of their first meeting and subsequent marriage was sweet and banal. Diana was a clumsy waitress at an elegant wedding banquet in Connecticut, James the best man. Waitress spills red wine on best man's white shirt. Best man catches enticing German accent in waitress's apology.

Diana accepts invitation to lunch in the city, another lunch, a dinner or two. Sleeps with James in between and parallel to other men – she never cared who she slept with. But he wants to marry her, finds her statuesque, Nordic and impressively aloof. She doesn't mind. There is a wedding (at which she notices him eyeing a young Swedish waitress). Diana becomes Mrs Painter, and very little else. Very shortly after, she is diagnosed with lung cancer.

This is where I come in. Their Greenwich house was, for me, a fairy-tale mansion, with beautifully arranged, barely inhabited spaces everywhere you looked. No noise or sound anywhere, except for the occasional subdued, measured conversations between James and Diana, and a lot of Brahms. For some reason, James was a Brahms fan.

This changed with my arrival. Diana wanted to be herself again, at least as long as she had the strength. She asked me to organize parties (she'd made a few friends before she married James), in the house, on the lawn, by the pool, in various rooms . . . We filled the airy rooms with obnoxious strangers, with loud thumping funky music, with food leftovers and empty bottles, with dirty sheets and strangely compatible smells and scents. Diana dictated, I only performed and enjoyed the task to the full. And she wouldn't stop smoking, even as she kept getting worse. I never nagged her about it. That was the first really rotten thing I'd ever done.

James became a stolid observer of the whole scene, always polite to the guests but obviously pained by it all. Until he started using the parties to his own advantage, supplying quality drugs and certain women that went with them. Taking those women to his and Diana's bedroom, whether or not she was there. Taking other women, Diana's friends. Then one day he took me.

I knew Diana had seen the move, and I remember the almost imperceptible hint of a benevolent smile around her tired eyes. She sort of nodded in my direction, looking straight at me, not at James. It felt like a very weird and slightly sickening stamp of approval. She seemed to be saying: OK, I'm dying. So just replace me when I'm gone.

OK, I'm lying. The entire preceding paragraph is a lie. I did go into the bedroom with James, but Diana didn't see us. Nor would she have approved if she had. When she gave me her ring, a few months later, it wasn't because she wanted me to marry her husband after she was gone. It was meant to be something to remember her by.

James practically raped me. No, I'm lying again. When he closed the door and gently pushed me towards their perfectly made-up bed, I was so aroused and excited I had to pretend I was completely passive, without a will of my own. I had to make believe it wasn't real. That I wasn't really there, that I wasn't involved in this disgusting situation. But boy was I involved. Some men turn out to be much warmer to the touch than you'd suspect. And I, by the way, was technically still a virgin.

Why can't I tell a straight story? James never, ever tried to touch me while Diana was still alive. It was all my doing. I resented all those arrogant, red-eyed women he kept bringing into their bedroom. Not that I had any claim on him; he was Diana's husband and I was only there to keep her company for a few months. Which, somehow, turned into a year.

Diana and I had a slightly unusual relationship. We knew pretty much everything about each other, including what we thought of each other's breasts, but we never really talked that much. Silent smoking partners. At some point in our adolescence, we became acutely aware of one another's presence. From that day on, we mattered to each other, even when we were apart. But I wouldn't call it love. I wouldn't even, in hindsight, call it friendship. You can live parallel lives without qualifying as a friend.

In New York, I found an emaciated but not uncheerful Diana. She didn't care much if she died, she declared drily as soon as we were alone. She had become a bit of a mystic. She was absolutely convinced she could start again, in another life. With parents who didn't have to pretend they were English every time they travelled outside of Germany.

The parties were meant to be a sound barrier between her mind and the world outside. Her cancer was too far gone for treatment, so we had nothing to do but wait. I thought she wanted to talk, but she didn't. Almost overnight, she had jumped a couple of decades into her unlived years and become a sort of incandescent middle-aged beauty, holding court to a pretty surreal crowd. When she died in her own bed, a year after I came, she didn't even squeeze my hand.

After the funeral – only James, a few friends and me – I went back to the house to pack. James stood in the doorway, watching me.

Then he said:

'One last fuck.'

He sucked my finger with Diana's ring on it. He made me say things in German. He always had a supply of coke for me. Eventually, he married me and then, when we moved to Chelsea, he bought me my first dog. It was a dark brown boxer, and today I have its clone. Now that James sleeps in his study Freddy and I share the big bed.

I keep waiting for this story to start being about me. *Really* about me. But maybe it never was and never will be.

After Diana's death, I made a conscious decision to forget her. I thought it would be a reasonable thing to do. But everything kept reminding me of her. Her clothes. Her dishes. Her ring. Her husband.

James was as cold to me as he was to the rest of the world. Occasionally, I would catch his attention, and he would be all over me. But not often. That's why he bought me the dog.

The coke was, initially, good for me. It helped me get through the day, and it made me write. James knew it. He also knew that my English was even worse than Diana's. So after two years in New York, he agreed to pay for a couple of very expensive language courses. But I learned more from walking Freddy's predecessor round the block, talking to the same people every day.

Then he sent me on a creative writing course with a pudgy guy called Joshua Engel. Engel thought my writing was 'beautifully truncated'. He told me to get rid of most of the dialogue. I didn't know what he meant, but did as I was told. When I wrote a story about James and Diana, Engel published it in one of his anthologies.

James was pleased, to my great surprise. He liked it. He set up a proper study for me, with a real Victorian desk, a dark green desklamp, and a portrait of his fierce-looking great-grandfather right above it. The desk had a glass top, perfect for my little habit. He expected me to go on writing until I had produced a book of stories about him, about Diana, about him and Diana. Not about me.

He invited Engel for dinner one night. I sat silent while the two of them talked about my writing, which, according to Engel, was becoming more and more truncated and therefore more and more publishable. He said some of his other students were starting to imitate my style. The chopped-up quality of my sentences, Engel said, obviously came from my interestingly foreign use of English. James disagreed. He thought it was due to my lack of focused intelligence. He didn't mention the coke.

My writing served an unexpected secondary and very useful function. When I reread it, I suddenly saw a picture of James which was a picture of Diana which was a picture of me. The writing wasn't truncated, it was just very, very bad. Engel was an idiot. But the portrait of the three-headed monster that eventually emerged from my efforts – James the sick devourer of young foreign women, Diana the self-destructive phantom/siren, and me: the self-centred, hyperactive drug addict, husband-snatcher, cold writer in a truncated foreign language.

Then, one day, I found a fairly decent reflection of a bit of New York in one of my stories. Nothing mind-boggling, nothing to put a sound track to, just a little paragraph about a mugger. I kept him on the page until he felt real, and for the the first time, experimented with some dialogue. Or, rather, monologue, because the mugger talked without expecting an answer. Pull it off, pull it off, he said. I pretended to struggle with the ring (my hand was thinner than Diana's), and then handed it to him. Just like that.

Unguarded

'So how do you intend to go about losing your virginity?' my father asks casually. He may have said 'getting rid of' instead of losing, I'm not sure. The dream then fades into something ordinary, like a swift walk down a deserted suburban street. Then into nothing.

I don't have a father. My birth resulted from a random moment of passion between my nineteen-year-old mother who was spending a summer as a foreign volunteer on a kibbutz in the Israeli Negev, and an Israeli soldier, also nineteen, who happened to be guarding the entrance gate one cool, dry August night. His duty involved a stroll between the squat kibbutz buildings. At three in the morning, my mother happened to be sitting in the window, stark naked, inhaling the crisp desert air and thinking with disgust of her return flight to New York the following evening. The kibbutz remained unguarded for some ten minutes that night.

Another option. My mother was skilfully seduced by

Tom Diaco, a close friend of her parents', during one of his regular summer visits at their cottage on Shelter Island. Mrs Diaco and my grandparents played cards on the porch, into the night. Tom Diaco, himself childless, hated cards and loved talking to my mother (or anyone willing to listen) about his writing (two superb mysteries and five very bad novels). My mother was flattered by his interest in her opinion, and did not mind his drunken groping for her body which seemed to have discovered a life of its own. While he made love to her, quietly, furtively, in her little bedroom off the kitchen, she fought off equal amounts of excitement and nausea by imagining herself as a character in one of his books. (The scene did, in fact, make it into a third mystery, at Diaco's agent's request to add some sex to the plot.)

Both encounters could be described as fleeting, arbitrary, almost non-existent. Almost fantasies. The older man had assured my mother he was sterile (hence his childlessness), and never again approached her sexually nor referred to the incident in any way (except by writing about it). She had exchanged no more than ten words with the Israeli soldier, in basic English; she had known his name (Tal), age and the fact that he would leave the kibbutz within a day. She never saw him again. Nor would she recognize him if she did see him; she has no memory of his looks and is not even certain whether he was fair or dark-haired. He was, she says, simply a tangible symbol of the unreal summer that was over. It was like sleeping with a ghost. Safety precautions semed irrelevant.

The time interval between the two accidental affairs had been exactly three days. Arriving from Israel, my mother had been picked up at Kennedy Airport by her parents and driven directly to their summer cottage instead of their house in New Rochelle. Diaco and his wife were already there. My mother, not beautiful but saturated with Middle Eastern sun and possibly already impregnated by Middle Eastern semen, was not easily overlooked by a middle-aged man who had known her from infancy. His sterility became somewhat questionable when he left his wife two years later and married his young typist, who gave birth to a son and two daughters within about five years. My grandfather is still in touch with Tom's first wife, but not with him, whereas my grandmother refuses to see old Mrs Diaco, though she communicates regularly with Tom and his new family.

Assuming that either man may have been my father, I favour the Israeli option. Tal was, and remains, an unknown variable. A mystery as to his genes, character, political inclination, aesthetics, relationship with God, temperament, taste in food and clothes, tone of voice. Material circumstances. I could be missing out on a lot of things by not knowing who he is. On the other hand, I might be very lucky. Suppose he is some kind of jerk. A family tyrant. A child abuser. An idiot. An unemployed computer expert, or a failed artist. A terribly insecure, inferior being. Or a man with a bulldozer ego. Possibly killed in a war (there've been at least two since I was born). All of this is nothing to me. I'm free of him, for ever.

Tom Diaco is now a wiry man in his sixties, but doesn't really look it. He has stopped writing literary novels, or at least publishing them, and has made quite a fortune over the years with his mysteries depicting the deadlier side of life in American suburbia. Although a lapsed Italian, he is rather Semitic-looking. Does talk shows and hangs out with the glitzy crowd in Manhattan. I see him at my grandmother's condo occasionally (my grandparents got divorced a few years ago). He is friendly, in an evasive sort of way. If I needed an energetic, egocentric, elegant father with useful connections in the literary underworld, he would be perfect. But I don't. I don't need a father.

In the dream, he is always faceless. Sort of like a talking shadow. He'd kick it off with an impertinent question like the one about my virginity, and if I don't answer, he just fades out, like the end of a video clip. But if I say something, anything, the dream goes on for as long as it takes us to talk it out. I like to wait till he's asked the same question a second or third time, which gives me time to think it over (I hope he doesn't know what I'm thinking when I'm not dreaming).

'Any suggestions?'

'Well, there are several possibilities. You could experiment, like your mother. You could see it as a project, to be completed by or on your eighteenth birthday.'

'Nineteenth.'

'Mm. Or you could wait for love. You know, the real thing.'

'Or I could just leave it. I mean, for ever.'

'Celibacy?!'

'Yeah.'

'But why? You're human. You have needs.'

'I'll suppress them. I'll channel them into something creative. I'll . . . you know.'

'You can't do this to me. My grandchildren have a right to be born.'

'Your *what*? Who are you, anyway?'

'Your father,' he sighs, and we part for the night.

I consider this a coherent discourse, so I write it down. I show it to my mother. She starts crying. My cool, cerebral, analytic mother. I just stare, waiting for her to stop. She doesn't usually do this in front of me. We normally try to overcome such moments on our own.

'It's just a goddam dream,' I say. 'What's the big deal?'

She looks up and I suddenly realize how young she is. Young, strong, and alone – except for me. My birth didn't really interfere with her studies and plans to become a psychologist (my grandparents helped a lot). She sailed through the whole ordeal (her life and mine) without missing a beat. She had guided me gently, competently, and now here we are, two grown-up people thrown together by mysterious circumstances. I had never really minded being so different from others. I thought of my mother as my own personal magician. Magicians don't cry. They just . . . do their tricks.

I guess she's crying because the dream made her think about love. Maybe she's sorry there wasn't any love in my conception. But I think there was. Even if it only lasted a moment. All conceptions do. My parents – weird thought – were just two bodies in the dark, mating, for no reason at all. But the attraction must have been incredibly intense, if it made them forget all about contraception. I can only imagine it as two people receiving each other in a completely natural, primeval way. Which would pretty much rule out Diaco. Please God.

Her voice is hugging me when she swallows a mouthful of tears and says: 'I did try to find him. My parents made me, back then. It didn't work. If you ever go to Israel, any man my age named Tal could be him.' She pauses. 'I wouldn't go looking for him, if I were you.'

'I wasn't going to. I have other plans.'

'Really? What?'

I don't know how to tell her. The answer has a lot to do with a tremendous amount of unrestrained, primeval loving. With a difference: I will not father any children I don't expect to meet except in their dreams.

The Gladstone Brothers

The Gladstone brothers, Simon and Dave, met every Friday morning at the BODY 2000 health club in Covent Garden, in order to destroy each other in squash or tennis, race each other in the pool, compare their muscle/fat ratio and brag about the week-that-was in their respective conjugal beds. The bragging usually took place in the sauna, or jacuzzi, and if there were other people present, Simon and Dave switched, effortlessly, to a simple code language. To an uninitiated listener, it would sound like a description of a slow, elaborate dinner at a trendy restaurant (Simon), or a quick one at the local chippy (Dave).

Their fierce competitiveness was a little unusual for identical twins – or so they had always been told by scores of concerned relatives and friends. But Dave and Simon weren't jealous rivals. They measured their strengths and weaknesses in a spirit of playful, tender curiosity. Observing each other's bodies in the gym felt like looking, lovingly, in a slightly distorting mirror. And they had done this since their early childhood; there was no real difference between today's mad race in the luxurious, kidney-shaped pool, under a profusion of lush tropical plants, and wrestling on the dingy linoleum floor in their parents' cramped kitchen in Streatham, when they were boys. Except for the fact that back then, their last name was Glattstein.

'Any luck this week?' asked Dave, as he emptied a bucket of water on the sizzling coals. The sauna was now almost unbearably hot, but even this was a part of their contest: who would last longer? They were both soaked in fragrant sweat. The Gladstone brothers' natural body odour was surprisingly sweet, almost baby-like, considering their substantial physiques.

Simon's response was a sour smile. The truth was that no, he had not been able to persuade Julie to even think about sex; but then, it was only Friday, and the weekend might change the picture. He wasn't going to tell Dave any of this, because he didn't have to. They always knew, more or less, what the other was thinking.

'That bad, ha,' said Dave, with a self-satisfied, fiendish smirk. 'Well, Valerie, on the other hand . . .'

'Jacuzzi?' Simon stood up, dropping his towel.

'Jacuzzi,' answered Dave, imitating his gesture.

This was a ritual. The first one to expose his nakedness, in the breath-cutting heat of the wooden cubicle, was a self-declared loser. But today, Simon wore an air of profound resignation. This didn't feel like a game, thought Dave.

They were not alone in the jacuzzi. A deeply tanned, chunky woman and a scrawny teenage girl – mother and daughter, presumably – sat between Dave and Simon, chattering excitedly in a high-pitched monotone. The older woman's indigo-painted toenails, which she exposed just above the surface of the green water, reminded Simon of Julie's feet: brown and pink, pampered, and always ice-cold. A classic symptom of poor circulation, and no wonder, he thought: Julie had become immobile, sphinx-like, almost mute. Not quite what he had bargained for, years ago, when he had ordered that whisky on the funny Czech plane, and she brought it to him with a beaming smile and an electrifying swing of the hip.

Simon and Dave had imported their wives from East-ern Europe, where they often travelled on business, after the wave of post-Communist revolutions. Julie and Val-erie were both Czech, which might have, at last, signalled a parity between the brothers. But Simon's 'trophy' was, by all standards, of a higher order than Dave's, for Julie was actually black. A native Czech Black: her father, an American, had visited Prague in the 1960s to sing in a guest performance of *Porgy and Bess*. Her mother, then a young make-up artist, saw him every day during the ensemble's two-month stay in Prague, and never again. She had had a few letters from him, over the years, even money. But he was married, with five other children and a show-biz career in tatters. So Julie's mother had raised her on her own, trying to shield her from constant racist mockery and teasing. She told Julie, who was possibly the only black child in all of Prague, that her father had been the main star of the musical, even though he was a minor member of the chorus. She encouraged her to tell everyone that she was American, and paid for an expensive English tutor. Julie inherited her father's fine singing voice, but she lacked confidence and felt no need to perform. All she wanted to do was hide from the world, become invisible. Working as an airline stewardess was not a bad option: flying from country to country fed her need to be in a kind of no-man's land. She fantasized about bumping into her father one day, or maybe even looking him up in New York.

Instead of her father, she found Simon, a taciturn British television executive on his way home from Prague to London. He was tall, dark and borderline handsome. They met quite often, in both cities, and everything felt right. There had been some awkward moments when they went out with Simon's twin Dave, who looked the same but talked and acted like an X-rated version of his brother. One time, Dave asked Simon, in Julie's presence:

'What's it like to fuck chocolate?' This was pretty clumsy, even for Dave, and he wasn't really surprised when she slapped him so hard that the red imprint of her hand on his cheek took days to fade away. They were the best of friends for ever after, and Dave's question was never answered.

Valerie, Dave's jolly, diminutive wife, had been a Prague tourist guide when he met her. Not that Dave was really interested in the city's cultural attractions; he was there to explore the possibility of buying some real estate and possibly opening a chain of nightclubs in selected medieval cellars. But his father had insisted, years ago, that he and Simon must visit the old Jewish Quarter, if they ever went to Prague. Their parents were now dead, but somehow their physical absence actually increased the urgency of that modest request. Dave could hear himself think, 'OK, OK, Dad, I'm going already.'

Not that he and Simon had grown up in what one could describe as *London's* Jewish Quarter. Streatham was deep *South* London, far away from the Jewish North of the city, with its stifling buzziness. They lived in a 1930s block of flats above a parade of shops, with an attached open-air pool – a haven, on hot summer days, for fleshy Jewish mothers with their poorly supported, overflowing cleavages and sometimes resigned, sometimes biting remarks on the inadequacies of life. But there weren't many of them; their small but self-contained community was only a miniature version of the real thing.

Mr Glattstein was a war invalid. His injury was emotional, not physical. He had been in the air force, no less, but when peace came he returned to his young wife a changed man, a recluse. He was fed and looked after by Mrs Glattstein, in a gruff but affectionate manner, like a third son. While she spent her days running a small shop selling oversized women's undergarments in nearby Brixton, to a predominantly Afro-Caribbean clientele, the father occupied the overheated living room, engrossed in card games and gambling with benign Brixton criminals. Simon used to hang around the shop a lot; he loved listening to the friendly Jamaican women, loved watching their hands as they touched and stretched the enormous bras. He would imagine their dark breasts filling the white cups, and found a strange sense of comfort in that image. He didn't dare peek behind the curtain, for he knew that his mother would ban him for ever. So he tried to act helpful, pretending to be interested in his mother's business. Sometimes, he would stand in the door and stare at the strange eel shop next door. He looked, transfixed, at the dancing, wriggling eels, and at their wild contortions when they were put under the knife, to be cut up for enthusiastic customers. 'Com'on, touch one,' the cheerful owner of the doomed eels would say to Simon, but he never did, and always turned away, hiding a deep blush.

Dave, on the other hand, loved to watch his father in the company of his rough, heavily drinking fellow gamblers, most of them graduates of the nearby Brixton prison. There was an atmosphere of merry camaraderie in their flat when the mother was away and Mr Glattstein had the place to himself (with his wife's muted consent). She always knew when his 'white trash buddies', as she called them, had spent any time in the house: it would be a stinking shambles when she came home, exhausted, from her shop. No one paid any attention to Dave – his father was barely aware of his children's existence anyway – so he would just sit in a corner, partly hidden behind a curtain, listening to the rich talk, soaking in the colourful curses and the pub-like smells.

Their father did have soft, lucid moments once in a while, when he seemed to revert to the talkative person he used to be, before the war. When this happened, he would reminisce about his Czech companions in the air force. There was a kind of love in his voice and in his pale eyes when he started remembering those friendships, which seemed more real to him than all the killing he had witnessed, more real than his own wife and children. It was in these rare moments of knowing who he really was, or who he had been, that he would say to his boys: 'Go to Prague and visit the Jewish Quarter. My friend Tomas said he would show it to me, after the war. Well, I can't go, because he's dead. But you can.'

Simon chose to ignore that plea, and when he visited Prague, he managed to miss the ancient Jewish Quarter, even when he had to walk right through it. But Dave had decided to get this filial debt off his chest as quickly and painlessly as possible by actually booking a special tour. Valerie turned out to be his guide. He took one look at her compact, utterly adorable *everything*, sniffed the balmy spring air around her short blonde hair as they walked together through the cobbled streets, and by the time they reached Rabbi Low's grave and Valerie was babbling on about the Golem of Prague, Dave had made up his mind to marry her. Time was of the essence: Simon had announced *his* wedding plans only a week before, and the heat was on. So Dave acted fast, planting an unforgettable kiss inside Valerie's mouth in full view of a stunned group of Hungarian tourists. He never regretted it.

The double wedding was, for a while, the talk of London. The Gladstone brothers were quite famous; Simon had worked his way, diligently, from a mediocre cameraman to one of the powerful directors of a new television channel, and Dave's crafty wheeling and dealing had, after all these years, somehow resulted in a solid portfolio of impeccable business credentials. Both brothers were in high demand at fundraising events, and would often lend their names, and their growing fortunes, to trusts and charities. It had been Simon's idea to adopt the 'Gladstone' version of the old family name; he thought it worked better in high-powered television and arts circles. Dave had no objection.

Julie and Valerie were quite happy to move to London. Julie's reticence was counterbalanced by Valerie's easy-going openness, and their friendship grew slowly but steadily. They would often sit for hours in Hampstead cafés, gossiping about the two brothers in Czech, trying to answer the burning question: Just how identical were their husbands?

'Like two eggs,' Valerie said during one of these intimate sessions.

They laughed, because in Czech, 'eggs' means 'testicles'.

'But actually, they come from just one egg. Isn't that a weird thought?' said Julie, sipping her espresso.

'And that reminds me,' she added. 'Do you know they have these so-called free-range eggs in this country? It says on the box that the hens that laid these eggs have the freedom to express *normal behaviour*.'

'Well, so do we. So let's get laid,' she laughed, slightly misquoting Dave's favourite phrase.

Their leisurely days were soon over. Valerie became an active partner in Dave's business in Prague; she travelled with him and helped him set up the nightclubs, with much success. They had a son, and joked that they would call him Golem, in memory of their first kiss. In actual fact, he was named Leo, after old Mr Glattstein.

Julie began to spend most of her time on her own, drifting in and out of a dreamy, half-euphoric, half-phlegmatic state of mind. Shopping was her drug, and Simon didn't mind at all. But it surprised him that instead of running up bills at Harvey Nichols or Brown's, Julie became a devotee of the open-air or covered markets, in different parts of the city. Her favourite one was Brixton, which she discovered almost by accident; one day, she fell asleep on the tube going south, and when she came out of the station, she felt compelled to wander around, for hours. When she told Simon, and proudly showed him the colourful dresses she had bought there, Simon said nothing. Then he mumbled a few words about his mother's shop, wondering what he would find there now. He hadn't seen the London he had been a child in since his parents died, years ago. Now, he and Dave lived in Hampstead.

But in the last few weeks – or was it months? – Julie had changed. She stopped exploring the markets, stopped shopping. When he left the house in the mornings, she would be sitting up in bed, hugging her knees to her chest. When he came home, late at night, he would find her in exactly the same position, as if she had not moved all day. He had no idea whether she had dressed and undressed again during the day, or whether she simply stayed in her nightclothes. The staleness of the bedroom air suggested the latter. The only thing Julie now seemed to be passionate about was the constant, obsessive painting and repainting of her toenails. She had assembled a vast array of nail varnish colours, and applied them to her smooth toenails with the meticulousness and the concentration of an artist.

Simon felt a slowly expanding sea of sadness in his wife, but he did not and could not understand its real depth. His own occasional melancholy came and went, with the soothing pattern of a regular ebb and flow, without leaving a deeper trace. Julie, he felt, was almost lost to him. He loved her, he thought; but who was she, and *where* was she? Sometimes, she seemed as far away as his father had been, when he was growing up without being able to reach him, to touch him.

But none of this could be shared with Dave, his carefree, joky brother. *His* life was in order, everything crystal clear, married to a woman who made everything fit. Just one smooth ride.

Or was it? Valerie was spending a lot of time in Prague

lately, with her parents. They wanted to see their grandson, and she had to help run Dave's properties. But maybe that was a handy pretext. Maybe she was sick of her life with Dave. Maybe even the generous, supernaturally tolerant Valerie had finally had it with her husband's hunger for everything female.

'You're wrong,' said Dave. They were finally alone in the jacuzzi; the mother and daughter pair were gone at last. Even Dave had had no devilish designs on either of them.

Simon looked at him, surprised. Wrong about what? He had just been thinking to himself. Now, his face was on fire. One annoying difference between him and his brother was that Dave never blushed.

'Wrong about me, and you,' said Dave, looking unusually solemn. 'So first me: Valerie isn't unhappy at all. She doesn't mind my occasional silly games, because, guess what: she plays them herself. That's the great Prague ethic, didn't you know? It wouldn't work for you and Julie, I guess, but it works for us. Now, about Julie. I've talked to her. Her problem is . . . well, it's you.'

'Me?!'

'Yeah. Because, she says – and I mean it's not me saying it, I'm just repeating her words – she says you just *stare* at her all the time, and you never tell her anything. You take her to these social things and you want her to look all glamorous, and she does. But she's known as the mysterious, silent Julie Gladstone, because she never talks. Why do you think she clams up? Because every time she opens her mouth, people go nuts about her being a black East European. She's sick of telling that story, all over again, every time. She's sick of being a freak. She thought she could get away from all that crap by moving here, but it's not working. So she just spends her time admiring her olive green toenails.'

'She told you all that?' Simon asked, suspiciously. 'And anyway, how is that my fault? I only married her. She can still have a life. She can get a job, or something. That's up to her.'

'Oh, I'm not done yet,' said Dave. 'You didn't even tell her we're from South London, until she mentioned the Brixton market. Why didn't you, Simon? I've taken Valerie to look at the old flats loads of times. In fact, I'm thinking of buying the whole lot – the architecture is pretty amazing, and very authentic, with that pool and those courtyards. In a few years, it will be a happening place.'

It was true, Simon thought. I do stare at her an awful lot. But that's just a stupid habit of mine; if I'm really fascinated by something, if I love it, I want to take it all in. That way, it's mine, mine to keep, mine alone.

'Well, that's just not good enough,' said Dave. 'Talk

to her, man. She might surprise you. Race you to the showers!' he shouted, noticing that Simon had had enough of his brotherly lecture.

'Fuck that,' Simon answered, slowly. He got out of the water and walked, with a deliberate step, away from Dave. It just occurred to him that Julie had painted her toenails olive-green that very morning, and never before.

'Simon!' Dave called after him, but Simon did not turn around. He drove home and walked straight into the bedroom. Sure enough, Julie was sitting on the bed, her head on her knees, looking . . . now he found the right word for it: despondent. Yes, despondent, but not lifeless, not scared. Not like a caged animal; more like a woman who has just slept with her brother-in-law, and enjoyed it.

'OK, talk to me,' Simon exploded. 'Why? And since when?'

Julie looked up, a bit bewildered. She didn't ask how he knew. She had already sensed a need in Dave to brag about this one day, as he bragged about everything. And while she waited, she let it happen again, and again, and didn't know how to stop: sleeping with Dave felt like sleeping with a very gregarious, communicative version of her own husband. But the guilt made her numb, froze her will to live.

'Since . . . I don't know. A few weeks. Maybe a

month. When Valerie left for Prague, and you were so busy every night . . . They have an arrangement, you know . . . anyway, it's over. Today was the last time. I told him.'

'But Simon,' she added quietly, 'the first time was a dare. I was a bit drunk. And Valerie and I always joked about . . . how . . . you know . . . we wondered if you're the same.'

'And are we?' Simon was surprised to hear his own voice. It didn't sound bruised.

Julie smiled. It was that same smile he had fallen in love with, some years ago.

'No, you're not,' she said, firmly. 'You're definitely . . . the tall, silent type. *My* type.'

Simon laughed, a light, easy laugh. So at least *that* contest's over, he thought, ecstatically. He moved towards her, cautiously. He wasn't sure how to proceed. What he really longed to do was touch her feet and warm them with his breath.

'By the way,' said Julie, embracing him with unrestrained energy, 'I found your mother's old shop. It's been turned into a trendy music store. I might get involved in it.'

'Great,' whispered Simon, and 'shut up now. Let me kiss you.' But then he stopped abruptly, fumbled for the phone and dialled his brother's mobile number.

The Gladstone Brothers / 167

'Dave,' he said, grinning from ear to ear. 'About those flats in Streatham? Forget about them. I put in a bid for the whole lot. Yeh, just now. Don't think you can beat it. We might even move there. Oh, and Dave? I'm changing my name back to Glattstein. No, I don't care if you don't. In fact, *please* don't.'

As he reached for Julie, he noticed that her toenails had been stripped of the ugly green enamel, and restored to their natural, bright, unpainted pink.

Beirut Lies

1

She belonged to the quiet part of his life.

When he finally turned his back on war-torn, bullet-ridden Beirut and landed at Heathrow, there she was, a light smile on her small, pale face and a half-hearted wave of the hand when she recognized him among the out-pouring crowd. The poet's wife has very broad hips, was Naim's first thought.

There was no car. She led him to the tube, and sat opposite him, still smiling, not talking, not even exchanging polite platitudes. Will she go on smiling when he finds the courage to tell her she is now a widow, as of this morning? Will she scream, moan, weep? Naim didn't think so. The poet had described his wife as a cool, middle-aged English woman, their marriage as 'real but distant', her features as 'delicate to the point of untouchability'. Naim had to agree: in the harsh light of the rattling underground train, there was a metallic coldness about her. And yet, as soon as their eyes touched for a brief split second, Naim knew that one day he would place his hands firmly on those generous hips, and feel their warmth.

He followed her like an obedient child as they changed trains, rode up and down steep, crowded escalators, and finally walked out into an unexpectedly bright, lively street. He had imagined a wet, grim, morose London, serious, restrained people under a grey sky. But he arrived on a sunny afternoon in late May, and as they made their way toward Francine's house, he was overwhelmed by the colourful mass of young female bodies. Unlike Francine's husband, Naim had never wasted his time inventing complicated metaphors for the things he loved: a breast was a breast, a mouth was a mouth. Joseph Haddad's poetry seemed to be all about wild flowers and immortal cypress trees. Joe would have described this oversexed London street as a fertile field of young wheat. Naim saw only nipples protruding through thin cotton.

But then, Naim was not a poet. In fact, he and Joe had very little in common, except for their love of climbing dangerously high, chalky cliffs and then diving, together, into the turquoise Mediterranean. They had first met at the bottom of one of those sea mountains when they were both in their late teens, long before their country had become a war zone. In any other context, it would have mattered that Joseph Haddad was from a wealthy Maronite family while Naim Hussein was a Sunni Moslem shopkeeper's son – but not there, not in that quiet spot they seemed to have all to themselves, so early on a Sunday morning. Pushing away from the rocky ground under their feet with just the right amount of force and tension, and plunging head down into the wet, bottomless pit was the most exciting thing they had ever done, the most exciting thing they would ever do. It was like a powerful drug that could kill them, but worth the risk if it didn't. Afterwards, Joe would lie on his stomach and write long poems in French or short ones in Arabic; Naim would just sit there, watching him, thinking how different their bodies were – Joe's was long and thin, Naim's stocky and muscular – and how they had smiled at each other before they leaped, not knowing whether either would survive the dive, wondering which one would have to tell the other's parents if something happened.

Naim's mother had come to Beirut from Tebnine, a small Shiite village in the South. He tried to remember Tebnine as the once peaceful, solid centre of close family ties and happy visits, not an unrecognizable bombed-out skeleton of a place. He tried to remember Beirut as the city he loved and never wanted to leave, a pocket of restlesss energy between the sea and the mountains, not as a ghost town violated by an endless war he never understood. He wanted to remember his friend Joseph Haddad as a lousy poet but a brilliant swimmer and diver, not as a human sieve he had been forced to abandon by the road to the airport this very morning. If Naim hadn't driven off, he would have been the snipers' next target. And with a hard-earned ticket to London in his pocket, the airport open for the first time in weeks, he wanted to live.

Their paths never crossed when they were kids, except for the diving. Joe's school in Ras Beirut was French, his friends other rich Christian boys. He was going to spend his university years in Paris, where he already had his own apartment. Naim was a mediocre, lonely student at his local Moslem school. He had few friends, and preferred helping his father in his shop in Ouzai, selling cheap souvenirs, postcards and shiny bargain fabrics. He would spend hours watching him play backgammon with other men in the back of the shop, soaking in the rich, sweet aroma of strong coffee and tobacco. That backgammon set, meticulously inlaid with a mother-of-pearl mosaic, was the only luxurious object his father ever possessed or cared about. Naim loved the soft sound of the tiny ivory dice rolling on the large wooden board, loved the smooth feel of the worn brown and cream pieces. After a recent wave of shootings in his parents' neighbourhood, Naim searched through the abandoned shop and discovered the dice under a pile of broken furniture, miraculously intact. They were now in his wallet, and would stay there for ever. He wasn't sure where his parents were, whether they were dead or alive. He would have to wait for the end of the war to find out.

He had left school as soon as he was able, and found a job as a trainee waiter at a hotel near Hamra. As it happened, he had made a lucky choice: the Commodore Hotel was used by foreign journalists and was very busy and relatively safe. While quite a few of his old classmates had joined various Moslem factions, grew beards, wore green and brown camouflage and put their Kalashnikovs to frequent use, Naim Hussein wore a spotless black and white waiter's uniform with a bow-tie and learned to carry heavy trays of food. He worked hard without sweating, hiding his feelings about his customers behind an impenetrable facade of efficient friendliness. But he couldn't conceal his delight when he saw Joe in the hotel lobby one day, in conversation with three foreign reporters.

They had lost touch with each other as the war escalated into uncontrollable chaos. Naim had assumed that the Haddad family would have made sure to be away from Beirut during the bad times, probably safe in their home in France. He was right – but not about Joe, who had insisted on staying in Lebanon. 'For my poetry,' he now said to Naim with a wink, 'not for politics.' He seemed to have grown even taller, lankier. He reached for Naim, affectionately, as if he was going to hug him, but then he checked himself and sat down again. The journalists, puzzled by the interruption, looked at Naim indifferently and quickly resumed their interview with Joseph Haddad, the poet who wrote about the war as if it were a case of brutal violence against nature, not human beings.

Naim had not been aware of Joe's career as a poet. But now that they found each other again, he made a point of asking him for his books – there were five slim volumes, one in Arabic, four in French. Naim couldn't really judge the French, but he was quite sure that the Arabic poems were immature, anaemic little things. He lied, of course, and told Joe he loved them.

Their diving days were over. They met at the Commodore occasionally, when Naim finished his shift or had a few minutes to spare. Joe was always excited, always full of stories, talking breathlessly from the moment they said hello until they parted. Naim listened, paying earnest attention to every word, but had nothing to offer in return. In spite of living in a city that continued to crumble under their eyes, like a huge demolition site about to be razed to the ground, Naim's own life was uneventful.

Joe's presence in Beirut was all the more surprising when he confessed to Naim that he had a wife in London. She was older than him, a small blonde woman in her forties, who had been his English teacher during his last year at school. They married secretly, in Cyprus, and would have told his parents about it if there had been no political tensions, and so many other things for them to worry about. She was a strange woman, Joe said, very quiet but determined. He thought they had loved each other madly when they had to do everything in secret, but as the mystery began to evaporate, apathy crept in, on both sides. Francine had suggested that they separate for some time, and went back to London. When the conflict became a full-blown war, she was afraid to come back to him, even though she claimed she really wanted to.

Joe did have a plan to leave Beirut at one point. He had reserved a place on a ferry boat from Kaslik to Larnaca, from where he would have flown to England. 'But then I imagined myself with her, in London,' he laughed, 'and I just couldn't go through with it. She would have been in charge of me – do you know what I mean? Here in Beirut, she was always a little lost, and I loved that, I really loved looking after her. Even though she'd been my teacher, and very motherly, we were on *my* turf. I was a man to her, not a boy. In London, we would be living in *her* house, *her* country. In a few years, I would look like her Middle Eastern gigolo. Here, I'm a poet, I'm *me*. I guess I need this Lebanon more than I want Francine. Maybe I even need this war. But I do love her. All the poems in my second book are about Francine, one way or another.'

Naim nodded, but did not understand his friend at all. If *he* had a wife who could offer him a safe, peaceful haven, he wouldn't waste his time in Beirut. He would get away, as soon as possible. He wouldn't care if she looked or acted like his mother.

He told Joe about his last two attempts to leave Beirut, both involving a risky drive to Damascus which he'd had to abort somewhere along the dusty road. Joe had an idea: next time the Beirut airport opens, during a lull in the shooting and bombing, Naim will fly directly from there to London. 'You can stay with Francine. Her home is my home, she always says! I will phone her tomorrow and tell her. I'm sure she'll meet you at the airport. How should I describe you?'

'Just say "a small Lebanese man with hidden muscles and big moustache,"' Naim had said with a smile, relieved – and a little insulted – that Joe was clearly unworried about sending him to his wife. Did Joe not desire every woman who slept under the same roof as him? Naim certainly did. Sometimes he wanted every woman at the Commodore, from the cleaning ladies to kitchen staff to the most elegant foreign visitors. Sometimes he wanted them all at once.

Joe had insisted on taking Naim to his plane. He didn't have to do it; the road to the airport was unsafe, and he knew it. If you could afford a ticket out of the country, you were likely to be attacked, kidnapped, held for ransom, shot at. The bearded, masked men who had blocked the road had a go at all of the above. They dragged Joe out of the car, tied him up and threw him into a truck. Naim heard shouts, curses. Then a quick succession of machine-gun fire, like an execution. He sat immobile under the gun of another masked man. There were cries of jubilation when they dropped Joe's body into a filthy ditch by the side of the road. Naim's man joined in the ecstatic screaming, taking his eyes and gun off his charge for a moment. That was when Naim stepped on the gas and drove off at mad speed, before they realized what he was doing. Several bullets hit the roof and one shattered the back window, but they didn't pursue him. He made his flight, and kept his eyes fixed on the antiquated control tower in the middle of the airport during the shaky take-off, as if to block any unexpected change of instructions to the pilot. A smiling stewardess offered him a copy of *Al Nahar*. He covered his face with it and wept, quietly, for hours. Then he closed his eyes.

2

'So you're Naim Hussein,' Francine said softly, when they sat down in her living-room. 'Would you like a drink? Tea, or coffee? Something cold, maybe? You must be tired.'

This would have been the moment to tell her. Instead, he asked for coffee, knowing that it wouldn't taste the way it should. He had to kill time, and think.

Everything in her house was massive – high ceilings, vast rooms, enormous windows, heavy doors. No one would come shooting through these doors. Naim felt a sudden wave of blissful relief. He wanted to curl up in the wide leather armchair, forget all about Beirut, and sleep.

Francine brought a large silver tray with weak coffee and sweets. She faced him, now without a hint of a smile.

'Joseph sends his love, I'm sure,' she said.

'Yes. Of course. I was just about to tell you. He . . .'

'Wishes he were here? I don't think so,' she said bitterly.

This would have been his second chance to tell her, and be done with it. Maybe it wouldn't be so bad, he thought. Maybe they would comfort each other. He didn't know any other person who really cared about what had happened that morning.

But he said, as if trying not to pry into the reasons for her barely suppressed anger against her husband, as if he only wanted to politely change the subject:

'It's very kind of you to have me here. I will find a job, and I'll move as soon as I can. I know the chef in a big Lebanese restaurant somewhere in . . .'

Francine gave him a strange look.

'That wasn't the idea,' she said. 'Joe said you would stay with me until . . . until he could manage to leave Beirut. You can't work here anyway, not legally. Don't worry, I won't be in your way. You can have the loft room and the upper bathroom all to yourself. Come, let me show you.'

Naim recognized Joe's poetic hand in this ambiguous set-up. But was it well-intentioned or malicious? Was it a game? A test of his loyalty? Was he being used? He wasn't sure. Why did Joe lie to him, and to his wife? *Now* he would *have* to tell her.

But she was already halfway up the dark mahogany staircase, waiting for him. He followed her again, like he had done before, in the street, trying not to stare at the gently gyrating triangle of her hips and her surprisingly compact behind as she climbed the three flights of stairs.

'Here,' she said finally, opening the door to his room. 'I hope you like it. Sorry about the basic furniture.'

It was a room as wide as the entire house, but with a low ceiling, which was in effect one vast skylight. The furniture was far from 'basic'. It wasn't English, either. Francine had obviously taken care to create an authentic Oriental atmosphere, including rugs, an elaborately carved wardrobe and desk, a large bed covered with a heavily embroidered spread. There was even an open backgammon set on a low copper table.

Naim was about to say to her: 'Thank you, but, actually, I really must tell you, I should have told you right away . . .' when he realized that she was gone.

3

And so it began, his serene life with Joe's widow. She had given up teaching when she returned to London from Beirut as Mrs Haddad, and bought and furnished this stunning house with Joe's money. She was receiving a generous monthly allowance from a special trust Joe had set up for her, she told Naim. In return, all he wanted was to be left alone.

'I'm a kept wife,' she joked. 'Do you understand? He pays me to wallow in luxury, far away from him. I hardly ever hear from Joe. When I do, it's always a surprise, not always a pleasant one. I don't know why I still care.'

They lived like a couple, sharing meals, going for walks, shopping, out to restaurants. Slowly, she became more animated in Naim's presence, warming to his shyness. She felt so safe with him that she left her bedroom door open, didn't bother covering herself if he saw her coming out of the bath. Did she think he was gay? Had Joe told her that – yet another lie? Or was it an invitation? Did she want him to cross over that increasingly fragile line between their awkward friendship and his uneasy love for her?

She showed him the Regent's Park Mosque, encouraged him to go there to pray. He did, once or twice, but felt uncomfortable with its opulence, and the unfamiliar crowds. He also didn't really feel like praying; it reminded him of his father, of the shattered life he left behind. He tried to explain this to Francine.

'But you must not forget your parents,' she said with conviction. 'The war will be over one day, and you will find your family again.'

Naim nodded, but deep down, he knew he had lost faith. He couldn't bring himself to believe in a God that wanted you to die, but he had always kept this thought to himself.

Francine never talked about her own family. Her parents lived somewhere in London, but she had no contact with them. She hinted at an old rift, something to do with her first marriage, to a Jewish man. 'At least I married a Christian the second time around,' she laughed, 'and they're still not happy, because he's a foreigner. And they never even met Joseph.' She had had three last names: Francine Watson, then Rosenberg, now Haddad. Francine Hussein wouldn't be a bad addition to her collection of borrowed identities, Naim thought, looking at her small white teeth. They reminded him of the ivory dice in his pocket.

She found it hard 'not to be in his way', as she had promised when he first arrived. Although he had his own house key, and often came and went without telling her what he was doing, Francine would always wait up for him at night, asleep in her favourite armchair, like a cat. Their late night conversations, over drinks, had begun as brief, polite chats, and grew into long, intimate discussions about everything from politics to their taste in food. Food was an important topic for them, as Francine's cooking had gradually evolved from having no value aside from providing sustenance, to spoiling Naim with all his favourite Lebanese dishes. She learned to prepare elaborate, colourful mezze and almond paste sweets worthy of a serious restaurant menu, and watched him devour these with an expression of child-like pleasure on her face.

But Naim wasn't allowed to reciprocate, wasn't allowed in the kitchen, even to wash the dishes or help serve the food. She had to be in control, like a landlady responsible for feeding a boarder. Naim suddenly remembered, and understood, Joe's words: 'In London, she would be in charge of me. In a few years, I would look like her gigolo.'

Maybe this was now happening to him, but if it was, he didn't mind. He was so besotted with his 'landlady' that he could no longer sleep at night, listening for her breathing, or any sound she made in her room which was directly below his. Within a few months, he felt he knew her as intimately as if he had been her first, second and third husband; as if he had known her for ever. If he drifted off to sleep, he dreamt about her. If he closed his eyes, he fantasized about her. But when he imagined himself touching her, or at least telling her what he felt, he saw Joe Haddad. He saw him alive, laughing, diving, reading a silly poem about dying flowers. He saw him dead, face down in the road, a filthy, bloody corpse. As time went on, telling her the truth about Joe seemed more and more impossible. She was bound to find out one day, but not from him. And she didn't need to know that he had been there, that he saw Joe die. No one knew.

4

The peacefulness of Naim's retreat from reality was a lifesaving tonic, but not for long. Slowly, he began to feel as if he was being poisoned by Francine's consistently calm manner, which suddenly struck him as intensely irritating. It was like living with a sexy teacher you have had a crush on for a long time; she was maddeningly close, but still untouchable, and still your teacher.

Naim was convinced that Francine was not a good judge of character. Based on her own account of her past, he decided that she fell in love with Simon Rosenberg, her erratic university tutor, mainly because he generated an embarrassing amount of noise and controversy wherever he went. Joseph Haddad was, in Francine's eyes, not just a charming, dreamy Lebanese student who took her to a secret place in the mountains and kissed her tenderly under a cypress tree; he was a passionate soul whose romantic poetry made her feel as if she was being immortalized by a great, soon to be world-famous talent. He felt that both her husbands had a much darker side to which she was completely blind, until it hit her in the face, like a violent punch.

Naim was also aware that she saw him only as Joe's sad, self-effacing sidekick, mistaking his quiet strength for meekness, his caution and inscrutability for lack of personality. Talking to him was a bit like talking to herself; he never challenged her, only listened, and when he spoke, it was in a polite, almost deferential manner. He fantasized that she enjoyed his company so much that she caught herself forgetting about Joe, hoping that Naim would stay with her for a very long time. She didn't even seem to mind that she hadn't heard from her husband in months.

During one of his angry night walks through Francine's fancy neighbourhood, Naim kicked the trunk of someone's beautiful old magnolia tree, with so much violence that it brought tears to his eyes. He noticed a little girl watching him, terrified, from behind a sheer curtain. He knew what he had to do.

Francine was waiting for him, as usual. When he saw her expectant, benign smile, Naim ran straight up the stairs into his room, without saying a word. If he had stayed near her he would have fucked her to death.

'Why are you packing?' she said. She had opened his door noiselessly. 'Is something wrong?'

He didn't answer.

'I see. You've obviously heard from my husband.'

'Oh, no,' he said. Then he shouted: 'You don't know a thing. You think you're so wise, and you know nothing. He's lied to you, everybody's lied to you—'

'About what?'

'About me. He didn't send me to be with you, to keep you company, like a nurse . . .'

Francine looked at Naim in disbelief.

'What are you saying?' she asked, firmly.

'Joe never told me to stay here until he makes it out of Beirut. He never wanted to come back to you at all. That's the truth. *He doesn't like being with you.*'

'Is that all you have to say to me?' she said coldly. 'Because I already knew that.'

Now he really wanted to hurt her. He blurted out, without thinking:

'No, that's not all. I wish it was. He was killed the day I came to London. We were ambushed on the way to the airport. I was afraid to tell you. I didn't know how. Sorry.'

Francine didn't scream, or cry. Just as he had predicted.

'So is that why you never touched me? I was wondering.'

He touched her *now*. First those hips, just because he had always wanted to. Then all of her. It felt like diving all over again, only safer. *Much* safer.

'Well, Joe didn't lie,' she said with a delicious giggle, the first he had ever heard from her. 'You are what he promised me. He could never do this himself. But you knew that, didn't you? We never slept together. The great poet didn't believe in sex. At least not with me. So he sent you instead. He said he had asked you to do it, and you agreed. He said Moslem men were always ready to . . . He said you were slow, but . . .'

Naim wanted to prove to her, somehow, that this was yet another of Joe's strange lies. He wanted to say that he felt as if he hadn't known his friend at all. That, come to think of it, the ambush *did* seem like an execution, not a random killing – and what could that mean? And those 'interviews' at the Commodore – was Joe really *that* famous? He didn't want to speculate.

He locked Francine into his arms, and buried his face in her hair.

'Well, thank God the poet is dead,' he said, and felt no remorse.

When in Palestine,
Do as the Romans Did

The first thing Noa registered when she stepped off the small British charter plane in Eilat were the two Israeli security guards, in *Men in Black*-style sunglasses and suits. They tried to look serious, but their baby faces were grinning benevolently at the arriving tourists. Noa couldn't suppress a giggle; she had just seen the movie on the plane, and the resemblance was hilarious. They stared at her, surprised, so she apologized in Hebrew: 'Sorry, but you look exactly like Men in Black . . .'

'Is that a compliment?' asked the taller one of the two. She noticed that he was wearing braces.

'Definitely,' said Noa. Then it hit her that they were in their early twenties, and she in her early forties. She had been the same age as these boys when she left Israel to marry an English man – but that was half her lifetime ago. She'd have to get a grip on herself and at least try to act her age, Noa decided, as she moved towards the terminal to find her suitcase. She would have been pleased with what the two 'men' said to each other about her long legs, as she walked away.

After more than two decades of doing everything with and for her husband and children, this was her first holiday alone. Well, not quite everything. There had been that brief interlude with a robust butcher, but it seemed like a dream to her now, as if she had imagined the whole thing. A flimsy fantasy with an almost bloody outcome. After that, her marriage continued, but became somehow irrelevant. She and her husband lived two barely intersecting lives under one roof, in a sometimes friendly, sometimes angry way. She watched her children grow until she could feel their separateness from herself, even from her love. They would be fine, they would be independent, strong, irreverent. But she had done nothing all those years except be a firm rock of support to all. She drew little cartoons and funny sketches occasionally, but showed them to no one.

Noa had stopped going to Israel after her father's funeral. Her parents were buried next to each other in the Holon cemetery and she wondered if they continued to bicker affectionately under those shiny black gravestones, or maybe, who knows, in some other, more spiritual, less crowded place.

She had sold their small Ramat Gan apartment, spent several weeks sorting through her parents', and her own, old things, and then decided not to visit again. Her home was in London now; she had become attached to it the way the wisteria she had planted years ago was now a distinctive part of her garden, becoming more and more dominant each year as it spread its light purple clusters along the fence and the thick trunk of the apple tree.

When she realized that she craved a short end-of-winter break, she brought home heaps of travel brochures about Florida, the Caribbean, North Africa. But after telling her friends and family that she was going to Key West – all alone – Noa suddenly changed her mind and booked a week in Eilat.

So, strangely, Noa was now arriving as a British tourist. Her last visit to the Sinai had been so long ago that Nueba, where she and her friends swam naked in the cool, translucent Red Sea and made love in the hot sand, was still under Israeli control. Now, it was Egyptian territory, and she wouldn't even sunbathe topless.

During the slow drive along the winding road through the desert, the mountains turned a soft, peachy pink. Next time she looked, the pink shimmer was gone, and the same mountains were enormous black silhouettes against a fading sky. Noa wanted to sketch them, but by the time she found her pencil, there was total, pitch black, eerie darkness, unbroken by any lights – not even from passing cars. The taxi driver informed her, in broken English, that they were near a border between Egypt and Israel, and between Asia and Africa, adding that Jordan and Saudi Arabia were just 'over there'. But Noa was more impressed by the night – she had forgotten how dark it was here. In England, nights were made of a less solid darkness, never quite black.

As the car penetrated the centre of Eilat, Noa could see, even at this hour, that it was no longer the dump she remembered. Hotels, promenades, restaurants, shops, cafés, amusement parks – it was a compact but perfect little resort town. She would relax here, soak in the sun, and the freedom.

She took her sketchpad to the beach every morning, and, without attracting anyone's attention, tried to draw the daily cast of characters.

The very friendly, elderly Norwegian couple on her right were her first 'target'. The man's hand was always on his wife's taut, hard stomach, or her small, exposed breast. His skin was the colour of boiled lobster, hers of rich milk chocolate. Noa couldn't capture the colours, but managed to catch the woman's angular features, harsh when she was serious, smooth and lovely when she smiled. Sometimes they turned towards each other, on their separate blue beach chairs, locked in a long embrace. Noa looked away.

Most of the beach was taken up by a large Tunisian-French family. Noa tried to sketch them all, with their massive gold jewellery and unselfconscious playfulness. The women had lavish cleavages which they shook and carried with pride, like belly dancers; but they did not offer their breasts to the sun, like the Scandinavian women with their well-oiled, shiny pink nipples. The French men were like little boys, teasing the women, seducing them into convulsions of hysterical laughter.

Noa noticed that Danielle Steel was the most read author on this beach, in five different languages. Under a large umbrella, a middle-aged couple took turns reading her in Russian, never exchanging a word. Noa decided that they were brother and sister, without any evidence to support this theory, except for their strong resemblance to each other. But then she thought, so many married couples look alike, and don't feel the need to talk. So she sketched them with wedding bands on their fingers, in case she was wrong.

Israeli couples were only half-silent; either the man or the woman would always be talking into a mobile phone, very loudly; the men to their business partners about work, the women to their friends about what a good time they were having on the beach. Noa saw an opportunity for a cartoon, but it would take some time to make it as funny as the comedy she was observing.

While she was busy watching the miniature universe around her, which, within a few days, had become so familiar that she almost forgot her daily life at home, Noa was being observed herself, by several pairs of very male eyes. Three Italian men, sitting behind her, had an unobstructed view of Noa's athletic body, especially when she lay sideways in her deck chair, one perfectly curved hip in the air, sketchpad propped up in her bikini-clad lap. It was the pose of a graceful model, all inspiring lines and angles, and Noa's absorption in her drawing made her look more attractive and less approachable than if she had simply lain there, inviting admiring looks.

Every day, around noon, when the sun was at its hottest, Noa stood up, put away her sketches and slowly walked into the ice-cold sea. She had a trick: if she followed the sun's reflection on the water, she found herself in a slightly warmer line of gentle waves, and did not have to hesitate before plunging in. She swam out into the sea, a short distance, and then she simply closed her eyes and floated. The sea had always been her drug; it held her, carried her, calmed her. But it also scared her, made her think of sinking ships and drowning children. She didn't stay long.

'May I speak with you?' said a man's voice, hesitantly, when she returned to her chair and covered her shoulders with a towel. Noa looked up and saw a tall, bulky man standing next to her, but not too close, not close enough for her to feel his penetrating green eyes. Not yet. She smiled at him and he sat down, clumsily, in the sand at her feet.

His name was Marco. He had been watching Noa for the last few days, he said, but didn't want to disturb her, she looked so busy. What was she drawing?

'Just people,' she shrugged, as if it was of no importance.

'Did you do a picture of me and my friends?'

Noa had to confess that she had not even known they were there. Somehow, she managed to miss them. Maybe she had a blind spot for groups of unattached males.

She talked more than she had done in days, and did not mind. Marco's English was very Italian, music to her ears. He was one of the *carabinieri*, a special unit of Italian policemen working for the UN in Hebron. In Eilat for a short holiday. Too short. Noa was sorry for him when he described the stone-throwing, but Marco said he loved his job.

'My father was in the navy. I always knew I had to be a soldier. I like to serve-a my country.'

Noa laughed. She didn't know many people who actually *wanted* to be in the army. Marco looked hurt: 'You don't like the army.'

'Not really,' said Noa, but felt a bit bad. After all, he was risking his life in Hebron only because there was no other way of keeping the Middle East relatively peaceful. He didn't have to do that; he could stay in Rome and do something a little less dangerous than dodging stone-throwing Palestinians and militant Jewish settlers. So when Marco asked her to meet him later that evening for a drink, she agreed.

He was waiting for her in front of the Three Camels, an English-style pub above the beach front. Noa felt that he was happy to be seen with her; she caught him shooting appreciative glances at her, and triumphant looks at his friends who were sitting at the bar. She felt flattered, but knew that she would not lie about her age at any point, if it came to that.

The waitress, a pretty, bald girl with a pierced nose, came to take their order. Noa never drank, but didn't mind sharing a beer with this man. Their conversation picked up, easily, where they left off before. It turned out that Noa was wrong: serving in Italy would not have been the easier option for Marco.

'I would have been sent to Sicily. Too much Mafia there! Very bad. Very dangerous.'

'So,' Noa said, not knowing what to ask him next. 'What do you think of Mussolini?'

'I like him,' Marco smiled.

'You're joking, right?'

'No, he was a-good for Italian economy.'

He was still smiling, but he wasn't kidding. 'And you? Do you like Netanyahu?'

'I hate Netanyahu,' said Noa firmly. 'And by the way, he is very bad for the Israeli economy!'

Marco laughed, but confessed that he actually liked Netanyahu.

'Oh my God,' Noa said. 'So let's see what else we disagree on. What do you think of the Pope?'

'He's a nice man,' Marco shot back, with an even bigger smile, followed by: 'So what do you think about your Queen?'

'I don't care about the Queen.'

'Why not?' Marco seemed genuinely surprised. Noa decided to simplify her answer. 'I'm not English. I don't have to,' she said.

'You not English?'

'I'm Israeli. I married an Englishman.'

Marco seemed more interested in the fact that she was Israeli than in her being married.

'I like Israelis,' he said. 'Most of my friends here are from the IDF.'

'Even the girls?' she asked.

'No, not so many girls,' he answered, with a sigh.

Suddenly, they were joined, noisily, by two other Italian *carabinieri*. They had already had a few drinks and were curious about Marco's enticing 'catch'.

'This is Massimo, and Paolo. This is Noa from London, but she is Israeli.'

They all laughed, embarrassed. No one knew what to say next.

'What do English women think of Italian men?' asked Paolo, a small man, with a tiny moustache.

Noa didn't really know, but offered a polite cliché: 'Italian men are supposed to be romantic.'

Paolo was enthusiastic: 'That's true! But we only talk a lot, you know, but when it comes-a to the fa-a-cts, you know . . .'

'Hey, speak-a for yourself,' Marco interrupted.

Noa was intrigued. 'So what happens when it comes to the fucks?' she asked, innocently.

Paolo began to explain something about Italian men being shy, when he was interrupted by a quick speech from Marco, in Italian. Both men laughed out loud and looked at Noa in amazement.

'I don't believe you understood—' said Paolo.

Noa was starting to really enjoy herself. This was fun.

She almost forgot that Marco had said he liked Mussolini. But now she remembered, and determined to find out more about Marco's tastes. Paolo had a copy of *Time* with a picture of Saddam Hussein on the front cover. Noa pointed at it and said, provocatively: 'The Iraqi Mussolini.'

There were uncomfortable smiles all around, so she added:

'Would you support Mussolini if he was in power today?' she asked Marco.

He looked at her with new interest. This woman was no ordinary flirt, he decided, and admitted that no, today he wouldn't.

Noa switched topics, but not her belligerent tone: 'Which football team do you support?'

'Rome, of course,' said Marco with some pride. 'And you?'

'Arsenal,' countered Noa. There was a story behind her choice. She did it to annoy her husband, who was a passionate Tottenham fan.

Marco laughed: 'Well, that's another thing we can't-a agree on. Your fans were much trouble in Rome!'

Noa wasn't about to defend the behaviour of English fans. Anyway, she wasn't really into football at all. And she was tired. She said no to the next round of drinks and said she had to go.

'I'll walk you to your hotel,' Marco said, with enough of a twinkle in his green eye to warn Noa that it wasn't a good idea. Especially when he put his fingers around her silver bracelet and started twisting it on her wrist, sending mild chills down her spine.

'No, thanks, it's not far.'

She stood up, said goodbye to the others and turned to go. So did Marco.

They walked side by side, not speaking. Then she felt his hand on her hair, brushing it out of her eyes.

'I like-a your hair in the wind,' he said, gently.

Noa moved away, slightly. Marco was, clearly, a man in heat. The *carabinieri* must get pretty horny down in Hebron, she thought.

'I'll see you tomorrow at the beach then,' Marco said, unexpectedly, and shook her hand. She was almost sorry, but she loved him for it.

She nodded and continued to stroll, alone, down the crowded beach promenade, among families with children, tourists, street vendors. Israeli soldiers. She stopped at a gift shop and bought a roll of film for her camera. She felt like taking pictures tonight, there was something about this evening that she needed to capture, but she wasn't sure what.

Then, suddenly, she knew. As she passed a huge

construction site behind a fence, she realized that the workers were still there, working in the dark, creating yet another luxury hotel. An enormous crane lit up the sky, but the workers were all gathered in one group, engaged in some manual activity. They looked like East Europeans, probably Russians, most of them older men. Noa tried to look into their faces; she saw exhaustion, tired smiles, men who looked like academics on a field trip. She took a picture. The flash attracted their attention. She waved, they smiled back, and posed, laughingly, for another shot.

Noa was surprised to see Marco at the beach the next morning. She thought he had given up on her, rationally, and had joined the others last night in their search for female company. But he had actually gone home to sleep, he said. 'I was tired, like you.'

Noa was about to confess that she had not really felt tired, just a little bit afraid, but she kept quiet. She'd had a bad night; her back was burned and ached whenever she moved, and a mosquito had kept her awake, buzzing around her face for hours. She chose to sit in the shade this morning, to reduce yesterday's sun damage. Marco joined her, like an old friend.

'I like Israel very much,' he offered. 'I like the people, they're like us – direct.'

'But don't you think Israelis are aggressive?'

'No, they're not aggressive. They are open, they say what they think. Like the Italians.'

'Do you know any Italian Jews?' Noa wondered.

'Yes, and I don't like Italian Jews. I like Israeli Jews, but not Italian Jews. They are very closed, they keep to themselves.'

Noa stared at him. This man could charm her and infuriate her, all in one go. She was about to give him a lecture on some basic principles of anti-Semitism, when he surprised her again:

'I want to learn kosher. Can you explain to me kosher food-a?' And he took a piece of paper and a pen from his bag, ready to take notes.

Noa laughed. 'You are serious?'

'Of course.'

'OK.' She took a deep breath. 'You have to separate meat from milk. You can't eat pigs and any animals that don't chew their cud, and don't have split . . . you know . . . feet.' She demonstrated the chewing, imitating a cow, and used the fingers of her hand to show a split hoof. Marco was writing it all down.

'So – no pig. OK. What about fish?'

'Most fish is OK,' Noa said, 'except . . . well, just write no sea food.' Then she explained about the neutral stuff – '*Parve* goes with everything' – and added: 'And the meat has to come from a kosher butcher, because the animals have to be killed according to Jewish law.'

'What's a butcher?' Marco asked.

'Oh . . . he sells the meat, and kills it, too.'

'Ah, *macellaio*!' said Marco, cheerfully. 'My uncle is a *macellaio* in Rome. So how do Jew kill animals?'

Noa smiled. 'You have to make an incision, a cut, in just one exact place, to let all the blood out. There can be no blood.'

'No blood?'

'No blood.'

Marco seemed puzzled by this, but did not ask any questions.

'Why do you want to know all this, do you want to marry a Jewish girl?'

'Oh, no, I don't want to marry nobody. I was married already, that's enough for me.'

'So how old are you?' Noa asked.

'Older than you.'

She laughed. 'That's not possible, because I'm forty-two.'

Marco smiled: 'And I'm thirty-five, and I'm older than you.'

'Your maths is pretty bad,' said Noa.

'My maths is fine, trust me.'

So that was a compliment, the Italian way, she

thought. Now she liked him a lot. She realized, suddenly, that the beach was as full as ever, but that she was totally oblivious of it. She forgot to listen to the rhythm of the waves, to the French woman's cacophonous laughter; she forgot to compare other women's breasts with her own.

'So what could I cook for you, kosher?' he asked.

'Oh, you can cook anything you like. I don't eat kosher. Are you a good cook?'

'Very, very good,' Marco declared. 'Do you like lamb? I will make you lamb with *rosmarino*, garlic, potatoes and white wine.'

Noa pictured this invitation to Marco's place. He would seduce her, confidently, by serving a perfect meal, without touching her once. And she wouldn't mention Mussolini . . .

'Why do Jew pray like a-donkeys?'

Now he had her attention. What does he mean, donkeys?

'You know, they move, like this, back and forth, and make a sound . . . it's strange.'

'Can I ask you a question?' said Noa.

'Sure.'

'Do you think church bells are strange? Do you think going down on your knees to pray is strange? Don't you think eating the body of Christ and drinking his blood is a pretty weird idea?'

'Don't attack me,' Marco said, softly. 'If you attack me, I can't talk with you.'

'OK,' said Noa. 'What I mean is, you have your traditions, we have ours. You don't have to understand them, just respect them. You're here to keep the peace, aren't you?'

Marco laughed. When he laughed, his white teeth looked almost inviting, and Noa felt safe again.

'Come to Jerusalem with me,' he said.

'I hate Jerusalem.'

'So come to Tel Aviv.'

'I'm going back to London tomorrow,' said Noa.

'And when are you coming back?'

'I don't know. It might take another ten years,' she said, but knew it wouldn't.

'I'm going to eat a mixed-a salad over there. You want to come?'

'No, thank you,' said Noa. 'I have a sandwich right here, and I want to sleep a little bit.' Now she really *was* tired.

As soon as he was gone, she couldn't wait for him to get back. This was crazy. She had come to Eilat to have some peace, to draw, to think. To figure out what she wanted to happen in the next twenty years of her life. Instead, here she was, falling for a moderately attractive Italian UN policeman whose heart was probably in the right place, but whose opinions contradicted everything she believed in. But, here he was coming back, and she was happy. Damn it.

'I have a test question for you,' she said. 'Is a giraffe kosher?'

Marco wrinkled his forehead, consulted his notes, made some calculations on his fingers. 'Yes,' he said finally. 'Because it has – how you say – split-a foot-a? And chews like a cow. Right?' He was pleased with himself.

'Not quite,' said Noa, triumphantly. 'You're right, it's kosher, but we are not allowed to kill it, because we don't know where to cut. The neck is too long. See how hard it is to be Jewish?'

'That's unbelievable,' he laughed. 'And I have a question for you, too. Is a camel kosher?'

Noa was about to answer when she realized that she didn't know.

Now, it was Marco's turn to feel victorious. 'You don't know! You know everything but you don't know if a camel is-a kosher!' This put him in such a good mood that he scooped Noa up in his huge arms and carried her a short distance to the sea, threatening to throw her in.

Noa screamed with laughter, managed to wiggle out and ran in by herself. Marco followed her and she didn't resist when he touched her under the water, out of everyone's sight. Underwater sex did not count, Noa decided, and let a few things happen that she would not have considered acceptable had they been on dry land.

As they swam back, slowly, Marco resumed his inexhaustible quest for Jewish wisdom. 'So when is Jesus coming for you, the Jew?' he asked between his vigorous strokes.

Noa stopped in mid-crawl and faced him. 'What do you mean? Jesus is your God, not ours. He's not a big deal for us. Just a Jew who had a few interesting ideas, maybe, but nothing special.'

'So why did you kill him?' Marco asked her, with a sweet smile. They were standing in shallow water now, two glistening, eager bodies against a blood-red sunset. Noa felt a violent shiver, like an electric shock from her head to her feet.

'Excuse me?' she said, quietly. Then she almost shouted: '*We* didn't crucify him. *You* did that, my dear! You, the Romans! And you destroyed our Temple too, and everything else.' Everybody was staring at her, even the silent Russian couple, but she didn't care. After two thousand years, she could finally tell a Roman soldier to fuck off!!

'But that's not what it says in the Bible . . .' Marco was mumbling, but Noa wasn't listening.

She ran back to her chair, and, without drying herself, quickly started drawing a camel eyeing a sexy, long-legged giraffe. She suddenly remembered that the camel definitely wasn't kosher. She wanted to tell Marco, but he was still standing in the Red Sea, looking puzzled.